Panty Ripper

A NOVEL

OMAR GOODNESS

Good2Go Publishing

This novel is a work of fiction. All the characters, organizations, establishments, and events portrayed in this novel are either product of the author's imagination or are fiction.

GOOD2GO PUBLISHING
7311 W. Glass Lane
Laveen, AZ 85339
Copyright © 2014 by Silk White
www.good2gopublishing.com
twitter @good2gobooks
G2G@good2gopublishing.com
Facebook.com/good2gopublishing
ThirdLane Marketing: Brian James
Brian@good2gopublishing.com
Cover design: Davida Baldwin
Editor: Kesha Buckhana
Typesetter: Harriet Wilson
ISBN: 9780989185998
Printed in the United States of America
10 9 6 7 6 5 4 3 2 1

Panty Ripper

Tia Fields rubbed her eyes with the back of her hands trying to adjust them to the brightly lit room. Her head was spinning out of control and her throat was dry as hell.

"Tia... Tia, wake up baby! Are you all right? What in the world happened to you? Were you out there using them drugs, because I could get you some help. Janice son Tommy got hooked on them prescription pills and..."

"Mom! Mom, please... You know good and well I do not use no drugs!"

"Then why are you in a hospital room looking like hell? Look at your hair, baby," Tia's annoying, over exaggerated mother said.

"I already told you ten times. I passed out."

"Miss Fields, Tia needs to rest until the doctor clears her to go home. I'll stay here with her until she is released and then I'll drive her back to her apartment," Tia's best friend Millie interjected. She knew her best friend did not want to deal with her mother as she laid there in a hospital bed. Plus, Millie had a few questions of her own that she wanted to ask since "Nosey" was her middle name.

"Okay child, cause the good Lord knows that I could not live in peace with any child of mine smoking on no dope!"

Miss Fields kissed her daughter Tia on the forehead and then left the room rambling to the Good Lord. Tia roller her eyes up in her head and then gave her friend a weak smile.

"Wassup girl," Tia asked Millie while raking her fingers through her sweated out, mangled hair.

"Don't you wassup me! What the hell happened to you last night? You got some serious explaining to do Missy," Millie said.

"Trust me, you wouldn't believe me if I told you. So please just leave it alone. I passed out while I was out on a date with Omar. It must have been something I ate."

"Or swallowed," Millie teased with raised eyebrows.

"Aren't you confusing me with someone name Mille Deep Throat Jackson," Tia joked.

"Yeah, whatever Ho! Don't try to change the subject. Did this Omar character slip something in your drink trying to get a little something, something?"

"No! Absolutely not! Omar Goodness was a perfect gentleman and just for your information, my panties was already off before I passed out," Tia confessed.

Millie hopped on the hospital bed grinning from ear to ear. She folded her legs under her and then said, "Do tell... Was it worth the wait? Please tell me his fine ass handled his business and beat the hell out of that backed up coochie. Then later you could tell me how you passed out."

Tia raked her fingers through her hair again as she began to chew on her bottom lip. "Millie, if I tell you this, you better not say a word to nobody. Now promise me, you won't."

Millie laid her hands on the side of Tia's cheeks and said, "Tia Fields, your secret is safe with me. Now tell me."

"Okay... Okay... Omar Goodness is a beast!"

"Damn, it's that big Tia," Millie whispered looking over both shoulders with a smile on her face.

"Oh, oh, no, not that. Actually I never got the chance to see his dick," Tia explained.

"Wait! Now you lost me."

"Well let me start from the beginning because you might not even believe me unless you hear the whole story word for word in explicit detail. You ready girl?" Tia asked already knowing the answer to her question. Millie's smile confirmed her readiness. Tia laid her head back on the pillow and stared at the ceiling for a second or two trying to collect her thoughts. Then she took a deep breath, exhaled, and said, "It all started at dinner."

Finger Licking Good

O mar Goodness sat across from Tia sucking half shell clams out of the shell. The slurping sound that came from Omar's mouth had Tia fidgeting in her seat. Her panties were soaked with her juices to the point that she wanted to excuse herself from the table and head straight to the ladies room to wipe between her legs. Omar had her right where he wanted her. This was their fifth date and he felt that he was finally breaking down the barricade that she had built around her pussy.

Omar with heavy eye contact and a half shell clam up to his mouth asked Tia, "so what's on your mind, Lovely?" Just as Tia began to speak, Omar loudly slurped the clam off the shell sucking it straight down his throat. Tia's heart skipped a beat and her breathing became heavy. Her pussy felt as if it was trying to jump out of her creamed up panties and run out of the restaurant.

"Is it hot in here?" Tia asked fanning herself with her hand.

"Actually I'm as cool as a fan, but if you hot.... Take something off," Omar said smiling his million dollar smile and Tia's juices ran down her leg.

30 Minutes Later

Tia and Omar came crashing thru Tia's apartment door lip locked and hands grabbing and tugging at each other's clothes. They were in a sexual frenzy as they left a trail of shoes and clothes all the way to Tia's bedroom. Omar's body was toned to perfection. All muscle with absolutely no body fat. Tia's knees were already weak. Her last sexual encounter was with a little dick, two minute bozo so she was well overdue. Tia had the kind of body that made men want to rough sex her all night long and tonight was no different.

Omar had her stripped down to her favorite purple and black panty and bra set. He had waited too, too long for this night to come and he had every intention on blowing her mind with multiple orgasms on top of numerous earth shaking and toe curling climaxes. Omar lowered his hands, palmed the bottom of Tia's ass cheeks, and scooped her up off of her feet with ease. Tia wrapped her legs around his waist and let out the thirstiest moan.

"mmm....mmmmmm, fuck me please! Pleaseeee... It's been so long. Mmmm....," Tia begged and moaned causing Omar's dick to throb and stretch to its full length.

"That's what you want baby? You want me to bust this tight little pussy wide the fuck open, huh?"

"Yes, Omar! Yes!"

Omar walked Tia's clinging body over to the queen sized bed and slammed her on it roughly. She bounced on impact which caused her body to tingle from her erect nipples down to her curled up toes. Omar could see the yearning in her eyes as she arched her back off of the bed. She was silently begging Omar to thrash her until the sun came up. Omar reached under her back and unhooked her bra exposing her erect nipples that resembled fat little light switches. Tia grabbed her breast and tugged on her nipples. This only intensified the sensation that was screaming for a release.

"Oh My God! I.... I... can't take this shit no more. Just fuck me Omar! Fuck the shit out of me," Tia screamed.

Omar smiled to himself knowing his next move was not what she wanted, but exactly what she needed. Omar slowly crawled onto the bed looking like a lion that was about to attack its prey. He grabbed Tia's right ankle and roughly pushed it to the side. "Spread these motherfucking legs open! I'm about to suck the salt out of this pussy!"

Omar's threat caused Tia to let out a tantalizing cry. She so needed this. Tia reached down to her panties, trying to pull them off but Omar grabbed her by the wrist and scowled at her seductively.

"Do not make me tie your hands up; okay. Now just lay back and let me do what I do, sexy."

"Okay baby. Just hurry the hell up and make me cum before I die," Tia begged surprising herself. In her normal life she was much more passive, but in her sex crazed cobwebbed coochie frame of mind, Tia didn't have a problem letting Omar know exactly what she wanted and that was some dick.

Using his right thumb, Omar slid Tia's panties to the side and then laid flat on his chest between her legs. Tia bit down on her bottom lip swaying her head back and forth knowing exactly what was about to come next. Her mind was so stuck on what was about to happen that the first lick caught her totally off guard and she damn near leaped off of the bed, but not before Omar caught her in mid-air and slammed her back down into the cushion of the bed. Then he lip locked on her soaking wet pussy lips. Omar stiffened his tongue and dug it under the hood in search of Tia's swollen clit. It did not take long to find due to its perkiness.

"Ohhh... Ooohhhhhhh.... Ooohhhh... Oh my fucking God," Tia screamed as her body squirmed from the middle of the bed to damn near falling off of the side.

"Ohhh no! Getcha ass back over here," Omar said in his deep masculine voice as he grabbed Tia's right ankle and dragged her soaking wet ass back to the middle of the bed.

"I ccannnt... I can't take it baby... OH SHIT!," Tia screamed after Omar slid as much of his tongue that he could fit inside of her. Tia tried her best to wiggle and squirm away from the tongue lashing, but it was an impossible task with the strong hold of Omar's grip pressing her waist down into the bed. Her ass wasn't going anywhere. She was just going to have to deal with the intensity of the pleasure because Omar Goodness was not stopping.

Tia reached both of her hands out to her sides and balled up the sheets in her fist. She lifted her head up form off the bed to look down and see if she was dreaming or if this man was really that serious with his craft. Tia was surprised to see that Omar was already staring up at her with lustful eyes.

"Ummm... hmmmm... Ummm... hmmmm... Babyyy, YES!" Tia could no longer hold her body up off of the bed. She slammed her head back into the soft mattress and cursed loudly. "FUCK! FUCK! FUUUCK!" Omar could feel her body tensing up. Her thighs began to squeeze tighter and tighter around his face so he turned it up full throttle. He was sucking, slurping, and sipping on her pussy loud enough to wake up the neighbors. Omar slipped two fingers inside of her gushing pussy and massaged her G-spot with the tip of his two fingers. Tia's left leg kicked out to the side trashing on the bed violently.

"OH MY GOD! OH... OH... I'm bout to cum! I'm bout to... OHHHHH, I'm cuming baby... I'm cumming... I'm cuuuumming," Tia screamed as her body spasmed and her pussy squirted three times back to back all over Omar's bottom lip and chin. Tia finally let go of the sheets that she had gripped so tightly. She tried to push Omar's head from between her legs, but his neck was too strong and he became relentlessly attached to her tender hot bottom. The aftershock of Tia's powerful climax rippled through her body while her senses became numb from the pressure that was quickly building back up.

(slurp, slurp) "You like cumming on my tongue, don't you?" Before Tia got a chance to answer, Omar slid his tongue down Tia's split until it landed on the two fingers that he still had inserted in her massaging her tenderness.

"WHAT THE FUCK!?!?," Tia screamed as she lifted her head back off the bed to get an up close and personal look at the spectacle that Omar was making out of her pussy. The sight alone was way too much for Tia to handle.

Tia's bottom lip quivered as she tried to formulate words to come out of her mouth. "Ooohh... Ohhh... Ohhhh SHIT! I-I-I can't take no more!"

"Hum?" Omar asked without taking his lips off of her. Tia's admission only encouraged him to go even harder. He reached his right hand under the small of Tia's back and then took his left hand and placed it on her hip. He spun her around onto her stomach smoothly but roughly at the same time.

"OH!" Tia screamed in shock and caught off guard by Omar's maneuver and strength. Her panties got wedged back into the crack of her ass. Using his teeth, Omar went bobbing for apples; rather bobbing for fabric of her soaking wet panties. He caught the fabric between his teeth within seconds and pulled the wedgy out. Then he hooked his thumb inside of them and yanked them to the side roughly causing Tia's ass cheeks to jiggle in his face.

Tia drew a deep breath. "What is you trying to do to me? I can't... I can't...," Tia panted and then swung her left hand around and blocked her dripping wet pussy form the assult that Omar was trying to pleasure it with. This made the beast come out of Omar. He grabbed her firmly by her waist and moved it away from his target. The juices that leaked from Tia's hot spot onto the bed sheets pushed Omar over the edge. He growled like the animal that he was and then dove in face first.

"Ohhh... Ahhh... Ahhh...," Tia moaned while she squirmed and struggled trying to get on her knees to crawl away, but Omar's grip would not allow such a thing.

"mmmm....mmm...mmmm...," Omar munched and moaned inside of her sending electric vibrations through her body and just like that the surge began to build back up inside Tia's body.

"Wait! God-Damn baby! I-I-I," her words got caught somewhere in the back of her throat as her legs stiffened up on her.

"You ready," Omar asked with a mouth full of slosh. Tia did not know what the hell Omar was asking her, but at that moment she was ready for anything.

"Ummm... hmmm...," Tia answered hoping that whatever Omar was about to do he would just do it and get it over with because she was damn near seeing stars. Omar grabbed a pillow and shoved it under Tia's stomach tooting her ass up just enough for the perfect angle. He grabbed both of her cheeks, pushed them upward, split them apart using his thumbs, and then dove back in face first.

"OH SHIT! OH SHIT! OH SHIT! OMARRR!," Tia screamed clawing at the bed sheets. The room began to spin as Omar continued to viscously lap up the storm. Tia's body temperature sky rocketed straight through the roof as her whole body tingled then tensed up and contracted. Then Omar did something that blew Tia's mind out of the world. He... He... He...

"He what? What did he do," Tia's best friend Millie asked a little too loud and too thirsty for Tia's liking. Tia's story had Millie moist between the legs and fidgeting her ass around on the hospital bed. "He what Tia? What the hell did he do?"

Tia shook her head trying to wrap her mind around what she was about to say. "He ummm... He, he, he ripped my panties off right when I began to cum!"

"Oh My God... He didn't!"

"Girl yes he did," Tia confessed. "And then my whole body exploded and squirted all over his sexy ass face. I couldn't stop cumming and when I looked over my shoulder and saw him licking it all up, girl I-I-I-I..."

"You what?" Millie screamed.

"I fucking fainted. Girl I passed out and now I'm here in the hospital."

Millie covered her mouth with both hands with a shocked expression on her face while her pussy tried to jump out of her panties.

"Tia Fields are you sitting here telling me that Omar Goodness ate the hell out of your nookie and then ripped your panties off of your ass while you were cumming and that made you pass the hell out; like literally fainted?"

Tia squirmed a little on the hospital bed and then said, "I swear on my mama," and with that confirmation Millie's juices dripped down her leg.

Wild Fire

Millie was having lunch a few day after the whole "fainting" incident happened with two of her co-workers whom she had become good friends with. Their relationship was nothing like her and Tia's relationship but they were still cool. Millie was a red-bone, weighing about 140 pounds, standing at 5'4, and with a body to die for. Her only problem was, she couldn't hold water. She was the biggest gossiper in the world. Her co-worker Bria was what her closest friends would consider a bisexual that was leaning more towards the ladies lately. Bria's problem was that she liked every sexy woman that passed by or sat too close to her for that matter. Her co-worker Joy was more of a square than anything. She was the type that didn't want to do anything, but always wanted to talk about everything and everybody.

"Bria, who you texting with back and forth? You hardly touched your food," Millie said with her nosiness not knowing any limits. Not even her friends were excluded.

"My boo. If you must know," Bria said without lifting her head from her Galaxy phone.

"Who's your boo this week," Joy asked sarcastically. Millie laughed and then gave Joy a high-five.

"What you mean this week? Don't hate the player, hate the lames that can't satisfy their women so they come running to me and my boo is Sugar, as if you didn't know this already."

"Wowwww! You and Sugar back together? When did this happen Bria?" Millie asked being nosey as usual.

"Back together?" Bria asked. "We was never apart. I couldn't leave that tongue alone if I tried."

"Her tongue cannot be that good. Is it good enough to put up with all that drama that y'all two go thru?" Joy asked always being the voice of reason.

"Put it like this Joy... Sugar's tongue game is better than all ten of your toys put together. If you find someone with a better tongue game than Sugar, I'll personally give you two thousand dollars," Bria proposed.

"Male or female?" Millie asked quickly.

"It don't even matter. Male or female, Sugar will put anybody to shame in that department," Bria bragged.

"I don't know... I know a dude that made a bitch faint because his head game was so good. So until Sugar put your ass in the hospital, homeboy got the crown," Millie said and then took a sip of her sparkling water.

"Millie cut it out! Now you know ain't nobody get put in the hospital behind getting their coochie licked," Bria said waving Millie off.

"I'm serious. The way it was explained to me was dude did the damn thing so good that she gets light-headed every time she thinks of that night."

"What do you mean the way it was explained to you?" Bria asked.

"Let's just say the girl that passed out is an associate of mine and I'm the one that picked her up from the hospital that night."

"I'm sorry, but it has to be something other than the oral that made her pass out. I just can't believe it. I can't...," Bria stated as she shook her head.

"Actually there was something else that he did while she was cumming. Maybe that played a part in her fainting."

"Yeah it had to be. What else did he do?" Bria asked.

"He ripped her panties off like an animal right as she began to cum."

"HE WHAT?" Joy screamed louder than she intended to.

"He ripped her panties off of her ass."

"This is too much for me," Joy said placing a napkin over her food and then she stood up to leave. "Why do y'all have to always be talking nasty? I can't even eat in peace without one of y'all starting to talk about dick, pussy, and cum. I'm out!" Joy waved her hand dismissingly at her co-workers and then walked away.

"That girl need some dick," Millie joked.

"Or some pussy," Bria replied watching Joy's ass jiggle as she walked away.

"Cut it out Bria. You know Joy do not get down like that so stop it," Millie stated.

"I'm just saying... Every time somebody mentions anything sexual, she jumps up and leaves; every single time."

"Well you know she ain't had none since high school," Millie joked.

"Her ass probably be getting hot when we start talking about it so she got to run away before she wet her panties. She probably run home and masturbates."

"Shit, she is probably freakier than both of us put together. A dude once told me that the quiet shy girls be the biggest freaks behind closed doors," Millie added.

"But hey, what's up with dude? That's what I want to know," Bria said.

"Who?" Millie asked as Bria read Sugar's last text message.

"You know, The Panty Ripper. I wouldn't mind putting him to the test just to see if he could even keep up with Sugar's skills, which I already doubt."

"Girl you tripping! The Panty Ripper as you call him is taken."

"I don't want him to be my hubby. I'm just trying to see if he could make me faint," Bria said as both women laughed, high-fived, and joked about The Panty Ripper for the rest of their brunch.

Losing the Scent

W hy are you being a stranger?"

"I'm not Omar. I talked to you three days ago," Tia explained halfheartedly over the phone.

"Three days ago... Okay, now when was the last time that we saw each other?" Omar asked calmly.

"Please, let's not talk about the last time we saw each other. How embarrassing."

"So when are we going to ever talk about what happened that night, Tia?"

"I told you, I don't want to talk about it. Please, Omar."

"Okay, okay. So when are we going to get back to our unfinished business? You know you like left a brother hanging."

"Better hanging than unconscious, wouldn't you agree?"

"Tia, I just want to see you. Please stop avoiding me."

"Okay, we can go out to dinner tonight."

"Thank you Jesus," Omar joked.

"Just dinner Omar," Tia warned.

"Okay, that's fine with me. You know I love to eat." Omar's comment caused Tia to drop her phone into her lap.

She picked it up quickly and then said, "Pick me up at eight."

One Hour Later

Tia buried her head inside of the menu trying to avoid eye contact with Omar as the waiter placed the appetizers on the table.

"Are y'all ready to order," the waiter asked. After the orders were placed, Omar reached his hand across the table attempting to lay it on top of Tia's hand, but Tia pulled her hand away so fast that you would have thought that Omar had burned her.

"So you're never going to let me touch you again?" Omar asked with his signature million dollar smile.

"Omar you put me in the hospital so I'm sorry if I seem to not be in a rush to go back."

"Since you brought it up, I don't want you to think that I'm some type of professional pussy eater. You was just tasting so damn good that I couldn't get enough. Damn!" Tia squirmed in her seat. Omar's confession had just saturated her underwear and stiffened her nipples. The thin blouse she wore did nothing to hide her erect nipples. Omar definitely noticed so he decided to keep her on the edge.

"I think it was your aroma that made me lose my mind and rip your panties off. I'm not trying to be cocky or anything, but you might have been better off passing out because I was about to knock the bottom out of that pussy!" The look on Tia's face was priceless as soon as those words left Omar's mouth. "Hey, I'm just being honest Tia. It's something about you that brings the animal out of me." Tia shifted in a seat a little more and she could feel her juices dripping down her crack.

"Oh yeah, before I forget... I brought you a gift," Omar said digging in his pocket under the table without breaking eye contact with Tia.

"Omar you shouldn't have," Tia fronted knowing damn well she wanted whatever gift that Omar had for her.

"Give me your hand." Tia reached her hand across the table. "Now close your eyes," Omar said seductively. Tia closed her eyes as she felt the silky object being placed in her hand.

"Okay, you can open them now."

Tia opened her eyes and saw her ripped up favorite purple panties in his hands and she gasped.

"They started to lose your scent. I guess from me rubbing them in my face every night before I go to sleep," Omar said licking his lips slowly causing Tia to drench herself.

Tia shot to her feet. "Excuse me Omar. I have to go to the ladies room."

"Can I come?" Omar asked with a devilish smile on his face.

"Boy, no! I'll be back in a second. Behave yourself in public."

Tia rushed to the ladies room in a hurry. Every step she took caused her juices to literally run down her legs. She entered the ladies room and had to brace herself against the sink using both hands. *What the fuck*," Tia said to herself trying to get it together. She turned on the hot water, pulled her panties off, and began to wash her pussy right there in the ladies room.

Fifteen minutes later Tia walked back to the table and sat down. "I'm sorry about that," she said. The food had arrived while she was in the ladies room. "Looks good," Tia said trying to avoid Omar's penetrating stare.

"So shall we eat?" Omar asked with the biggest grin on his face.

Tia shook her head, blushed with a shy smile, and then said, "Let's."

Thirty minutes had passed and they had both eaten their meals. After all that food, Omar was still hungry, for Tia that is. "Tia let's get out of here. I'm ready for desert."

Tia almost choked on her drink. "Omar, I have a very important meeting in the morning; you know a career changing type of meeting," Tia said. Omar was crushed, but he didn't let it show. Truth be told, he was catching feelings for Tia which was something he rarely did, but he had no control over the way he had been feeling. Ever since he rode in the back of the ambulance with her to the hospital with her, he had been feeling some type of way about Tia.

"Okay, well can I atleast have those panties back until the next time that I see you?"

"What good are they if they have lost the scent?" Tia could not believe the words that were coming out of her mouth. Omar had really tapped into her freaky side.

"Well what about the ones that you have on? Can I have those? They will really help me sleep at night. Your scent is so intoxicating." Tia did not know how to respond. She could not believe that Omar had just asked for her panties that were already soaked with her juices.

"I-I-I," Tia stuttered.

"Let me handle it," Omar said looking around the restaurant and when he was certain that no one was looking in their direction, he slid his chair back a little and then dipped under the table. Tia wanted to protest, wanted to get up and run out of the restaurant, but she was too in shock and horny to move. Tia looked around the restaurant and she realized that no one was even looking at them. She jumped when she felt Omar place both of his hands on her knees. Tia pushed his hands away and then squeezed her legs together. Omar slid his hands up both sides of Tia's thighs until he reached the fabric of her panties. Tia tried to push his hands away without causing any attention to herself or Omar for that matter. Omar laid his face in her lap and even though he could not lick her pussy from that position, he could damn sure smell it which was always good enough to bring out the beast in him. Omar began to yank on her panties, but Tia pressed her weight down and squeezed her legs together even tighter. The struggle caused friction against Tia's clit and she let out a small moan.

"Ummm... Come from under... Ummm there," Tia said as her breath began to quicken while Omar continued to yank and pull. The friction was becoming too much for her. There was no way she could control her facial expressions at this point so she dropped her head into her hands. Tia bit down on the bottom part of her palm to contain any sounds of pleasure that was trying to escape her mouth. The tension started to build and Tia tried to push the chair back to escape, but Omar was too strong. He quickly positioned his index and middle finger gently against her swollen clit and began to massage it in a circular motion. Immediately he could feel her juices began to flow and all that did was turn him on even more. The tension was building, building, building and just as Omar was about to get into beast mode, it happened. Omar began to rip Tia's panties off as she came all over his fingers. Tia's legs began to shake and shiver as the orgasm began to rock her body over and over again for a few seconds. Omar was shocked at how fast he was able to make Tia's pussy explode especially since he called himself taking it easy on her.

"Excuse me Miss... Is everything okay?" the waiter asked after noticing Tia with her head down looking like she was chocking or something.

"Ye-Yes. I'm fine," Tia said after lifting her head up. The waiter walked away just as Omar slid Tia's ripped panties from between her legs. Omar came from under the table with a sinister smile on his face and Tia didn't know if she was more pissed off or turned on by Omar's actions. Tia avoided Omar's sexy smile and motioned for the waiter to bring them the check. Omar had Tia's panties balled up in his hand. He raised his hand to his nose and inhaled deeply. Tia's body shook one last time as her juices began to soak the back of her dress.

Ten minutes later they were outside walking toward the parking lot. There wasn't a lot of words being exchanged between the two of them, but the way Tia held on to Omar's hand tightly, he knew it would only be a matter of time before he had her begging him to fuck her harder. Well, at least that's what he was thinking as they walked. Omar was just about to try one last time to convince her to go home with him when he heard glass shattering and then a car alarm blaring in the distance. The more he listened, car alarm sounded like his own car. Then a white Dodge Charger sped out of the opposite end of the parking lot and Omar knew at that point exactly what was going on.

Holding Tia's hand, they jogged over to where Omar's black Escalade sat keyed up with a big hole in the windshield where a brick had been thrown. When they got right up on his Escalade they noticed that the brick was sitting on the driver's seat.

"CRAZY BITCH," Omar screamed and then pulled out his phone to call Tia a cab.

Party of the Year

One Week Later

T ia stop being a prude. It's only the biggest party of the year. You got to go," Millie whined.

"Millie you know I'm not feeling the whole club scene. Take your co-workers Joy and Bria with you," Tia said dismissingly.

"They are already coming and I told them that they'll finally get the chance to meet you. Plus how are you not going to show up to your man's birthday bash?"

"Girl pleaseee... Omar Goodness is not my man and speaking of Omar's ass, he took me out to dinner last week and..."

"Ummm," Millie moaned with a smile.

"Ummm what? I didn't give him none if that's what you're thinking, but listen to this. While we were in the restaurant, somebody keyed his car and threw a brick through his window."

"Sounds like a crazy ex. Somebody's missing that thunder tongue that you are so scared of," Millie joked.

"I'm not scared of him. He's just... Just..."

"Oh my gosh! Look at you blushing Miss Tia Fields, and he's just what?" Millie's nosey ass asked.

Tia shook her head. "You better not say nothing."

"Whattttt? You got the dick?" Millie asked excitedly.

Tia roller her eyes at her best friend who seemed to have a one track mind. "Noooo, but I can't believe I'm about to tell you this."

"Tell me," Millie begged.

"When we was inside the restaurant, Omar crawled under the table and..." Tia shook her head and then blurted it out. "He crawled under the table, ripped my panties off, and gave me the best finger fucking that I ever had in my life!"

Millie's jaw dropped causing her mouth to form the letter 'O' as her own pussy began to twitch. "Wowwww! That's so kinky and dirty! He's a panty ripping freak!" The two women giggled like high school girls.

"Oh you are so going to this party," Millie said grabbing Tia's hand and pulling her off of the bed.

Ripping Lace

Omar turned into the driveway of the two story house on the quiet residential block. The rental car that he was driving was an insult to his swag, but there was no way in the world he would drive his Escalade to see the same sex crazed nympho that had vandalized it in the first place. It was bad enough that she threatened to crash his party if he didn't come to see her immediately. She said her reason for needing to see him was because she needed to talk to him about a serious matter. That alone had Omar on the edge because she never wanted to talk. All she ever wanted to do was have sex, rough sex at that.

Omar rang the doorbell repeatedly and was clearly annoyed with the whole ordeal. He had three hours before he had to be at his birthday bash and he really didn't have time for a long conversation. Finally, the door swung open and there she stood looking like a brown skin Egyptian Goddess wearing a silk robe. She smiled and then stepped to the side.

"Let's make this quick. I wouldn't want to be late to my own party," Omar said.

"Okay handsome, we'll skip the foreplay this time. Who's pussy was it that you ate so good that the bitch fainted?" Her question caught Omar off guard. He started to lie, but what was the sense in that? It was obvious that she already knew what she was talking about. He just couldn't understand how she found out that bit of information.

"Who told you that," he fumed.

"Not important. Who is she Omar," she said calmly.

"I don't owe you an explanation! Stay the hell out of my business!"

"That dick and that tongue is my business!"

Omar charged her, grabbing her by the throat and squeezing tightly.

"Why the fuck did you violate my truck? Huh?"

"To-to-to make you mad," she said struggling for air.

"And why the fuck would you want to make me mad? Huh?"

"So you ca-ca-could FUCK THE SHIT OUT OF ME," she screamed as best she could.

"Oh yeah! That's whay you want, you crazy bitch?"

"Yes big daddy. Yessss!" Omar slammed her back against the wall knocking some of the photos off the wall and a framed diploma. Using his other hand, he roughly snatched her robe off. Her black lace panty and bra set looked very nice and expensive which caused Omar's dick to swell up instantly. She knew what was going through his mind. She had seen that same look in his eyes a many of times.

"You better not Omar! These are my favorite ones," she lied. "I love these like you love your truck."

Omar's inner beast roared and he scooped her up off her feet and slung her over his right shoulder. He walked up the stairs to her closed bedroom door and kicked the door open with his foot. "BOOM!"

"Oh my, big daddy don't hurt this pussy," she screamed knowing that's exactly what she wanted him to do. Omar smacked her on the ass hard causing her to yelp in pain and pleasure.

"You asked for it, you nasty little bitch and now you are going to get it," Omar said smacking on the ass again, but even harder this time. Her ass cheek jiggled against the side of his face exciting him. Using both hands, Omar reached up and dug his fingers through her lace panties and began to rip them to shreds. The sound of the lace being ripped was Omar's trigger. He slammed her on the bed and peeled his clothes off in seconds. She turned over onto her stomach and looked over her shoulder as Omar climbed onto the bed.

"I'm sorry for wrecking your truck big daddy, but it felt soooo fucking good doing it," she said. She was really trying to get her brains fucked out by pissing him off. Omar shoved her face into the pillows that were on the bed. He was tired of hearing her mouth. Without warning, Omar entered her forcefully. A muffled scream came from the pillows. Her pussy was already soaking wet due to all of his roughness. Omar continued his thrusting until all she could hear and feel were his balls smacking loudly against her hot and wanting ass.

"Bitch, if you ever fuck with my ride again," Omar growled.

She struggled to get her head out of the pillows and screamed, "I'M SORRY! FUCK ME HARDER! FUCK ME HARDER! PUNISH THIS PUSSY!" And that's exactly what Omar did. He pushed her head back down into the pillows and continued to pound in and out of her.

"Shut the fuck up and take this dick; this whole motherfucking dick," Omar said as he pounded her like he wanted to break his whole ten inches off in her. Omar needed to see her face. He stopped for a few minutes and turned her over. "I'm gonna teach you about fucking with me," he said. He reached over and picked up her ripped up panties. He knew from their previous sexcapades that she was beyond flexible. Omar grabbed her by both ankles and brought them both together. Then using her ripped panties, he tied both of her ankles together.

"Wh-what are you doing big daddy?" Omar lightly smacked her in the face knowing that she loved that rough shit.

"Didn't I say shut up!"

"Yes big daddy. I'm sorry. I'm just soooo wet," she screamed.

Omar grabbed her by the ankles bent her legs all the way back. Then he lifted her head a little until her ankles were literally stuck behind her head. He admired his artwork as she laid there folded up with her pussy poking out. With no legs in his way, Omar positioned himself to enter her and with one hard thrust, he did.

"Oooohhhhh fuck! Yes big daddy, fuck me like you mad at me! Fuck me like you hate me!" she screamed. "Ummm... uuummmmm," she moaned as Omar continued to pound her pussy.

"Shut your fucking mouth and take this dick," Omar said aggressively.

"NO!" she screamed trying to make Omar go harder and deeper and that he did. "Aaarrrrgh!"

"Oh shit! Oh shit big daddy! I'mma cum! I'm about to cum! I'mma... OOOHHHHH, I'M CUMMMMING," she screamed as her whole body shook and shook and shook.

Omar Goodness' Birthday Bash

Three hours later Omar Goodness walked into club 'Cas-U-Al' decked out in a black Armani suit with a pair of Gucci loafers on his feet. His low haircut made his waves look as if he was born with them. The dim lighting in the club complemented his chocolate complexion and his smile was the absolute definition of a Colgate smile. Women whispered and pointed as the young black entrepreneur made his way to the V.I.P. section where family, friends, and a few of his top employees awaited him.

"Omar Goodness get your butt over here and give your favorite cousin a hug. You know I got my goodies on."

Omar laughed. "Too much information cuz, but thanks for all the support." 'Goodies' was Omar's silk lace panty line that took the world by storm making him an overnight success and millionaire. A friend of Omar's passed him a bottle of champagne and a Cuban cigar. Omar accepted it and walked over to the see-through glass that over looked the dance floor. As soon as his figure appeared in front of the glass, a few party goers pointed up at him. Omar raised both his hands in the air and did a quick little two step to the music.

After two good hours of partying hard and having a ball, Omar sat at his table talking with two of his best boys, Kinard and Askari.

"So who is this mystery lady and when do we get to meet her?" Kinard asked with a smile.

"As soon as she gets here. Her name is Tia and she's no mystery. She's the real thing," Omar replied.

"Damn! Not my man Mr. Omar Goodness sounding all pussy whipped. Let me find out," Askari joked.

"There you go talking crazy. Omar Goodness don't get pussy whipped. I whip that pussy," Omar said.

"Man I don't understand you two," Kinard stated. "Women are God's best creation, not what' between their legs." Kinard was what you would consider the perfect gentleman who had absolutely no luck with the ladies. He could not understand how Omar and Askari had a handful of perfect woman each and he could not find a half decent one to save his life.

"Askari, how many times do I have to explain this to you bro? Women love sex more than men. They are animals. If there was an epidemic that eliminated all hard-ons causing every man in the world to be forever limp, do you know how fast the suicide rate for women would rise?" Omar yelled over the music causing him and his two buddies to bust out laughing until their conversation was interrupted by one of the bouncers.

"Excuse me Omar, but you have a Ms. Tia Fields and one guest trying to gain access to the V.I.P. area."

"Speaking of the angel herself," Omar said smiling at Askari and Kinard. "Let them in, please." The bouncer left and within seconds Tia and Millie came walking up looking like they had just stepped out of a photo shoot. They were decked out in the latest fashion which only complimented their natural beauty.

Omar stood to greet his guest. "Hello birthday boy," Tia said smiling as she walked into Omar's embrace.

"Hey beautiful. I'm so glad you could make it," Omar said.

"Wouldn't have missed it for the world," Tia lied knowing good and well that it was Millie who dragged her to the party. Millie cleared her throat wanting to be introduced to the beast that made her friend faint by pleasing her orally.

"Oh, how rude of me," Tia said. "Omar, this is my best friend Millie. Millie this is Mr. Omar Goodness." Omar smiled as him and Millie shook hands.

"Any friend of Tia's is a friend of mine," Omar said ending their handshake. Omar's hands were soft, but strong and Millie's pussy got moist just from his touch. Millie could not take her eyes off of Omar's mouth as he spoke.

"Hello Omar. I've heard a lot about you." Tia wanted to pinch Millie for her indirect comment.

"Oh really? I hope it was all good," Omar said and then licked his lips without any seduction intended. "Well let me introduce you two beautiful women to some close friends of mine," Omar said. Askari and Kinard stood as the formal introductions were made. Millie barely looked in their direction because her eyes were glued to Mr. Omar Goodness. Everyone finally took a seat. Omar filled their glasses with champagne and the conversation began with Kinard exposing their prior conversation.

"Ladies, quick question," Kinard said before he took a sip of his drink and continued. "Can a man be perfect, and when I say perfect, I mean the man of your dreams perfect and be impotent at the same time?" Tia almost choked off of her champagne causing Omar to pat her on the back.

"Well judging by Tia's panic attack, I guess it will be safe to assume that a man cannot be anywhere near remotely perfect if he can't produce a hard-on for his lady," Omar added with a light chuckle.

"Unless," Millie blurted out causing everyone to look in her direction.

"Unless what?" Kinard asked hoping Millie proved once and for all that women were in no way as animalistic as men were when it came to sex.

"Unless he has one hell of a tongue game," Millie stated cutting her eyes at Omar.

Tia kicked Millie's leg under the table and quickly changed the subject. "So Omar are you enjoying your birthday bash," she asked as Kinard and Askari debated over Millie's oral sex comment.

"Actually I am now that you are here, sweetness."

Tia blushed and shook her head. "Boy you are too much," she said.

"And you only know the half. There's a lot more about Omar Goodness that you haven't had the chance to explore," Omar said. His comment made Tia shift in her seat as the room started to feel a little hot to her.

"What are you two over there whispering about, Tia?" Millie's nosey ass asked as her phone began to vibrate. Millie read the text message, turned to Askari and Kinard, and then said, "my co-workers just arrived. Would you two like to meet them?"

"Let's do it," Askari said already on his feet. "Where are they?" he asked.

"Downstairs at the bar. Come on fellas," Millie said as the trio walked off leaving Omar and Tia at the table by themselves. Omar and Tia never even noticed that the trio had walked away. He had Tia's brain wrapped around his tongue while the only thing that was on his mind was fucking her brains out until the sun came up.

At the Bar

Millie introduced Bria to Askari and Joy to Kinard. She figured Bria would have her way with Askari due to the fact that he seemed to have a one track mind and Joy and Kinard would hit it off quite well. You know with Joy being a good God fearing Christian woman and Kinard being the perfect gentleman. He believed that women should be treated like the queens that they truly were and not a sex object.

Millie was up to no good as usual. Her intensions were self-motivated as usual. She wanted to remove Omar's friends out of the picture which she had just done. Now she had to find a way to get Tia out of the way as well. In Millie's mind, Tia didn't know what to do with Omar Goodness with his fine ass, but she definitely did.

"Yall go ahead and get acquainted while I go mingle a bit," Millie said as she walked away. Millie's mind was working on overdrive as she moved through the throng of party goers on her way to the DJ booth. Normally no one would be allowed to enter the DJ booth, but the way Millie's dress hugged her curves gave her all access to whatever she wanted and whoever she wanted. Minutes later Millie was back out of the booth smiling from ear to ear. She was thinking that her plan had to work. She strutted back to the bar sitting a few stools down from where Askari and Bria were sitting. They seemed to be getting along very well. Millie ordered an apple Martini and just as her drink arrived, the DJ stopped the music and made an announcement.

"Can I have everyone's attention for a second, please? Can the owner of a red 545 B.M.W. with the license plate 832-X9L please head to the parking lot? You are blocking someone in. I repeat, can the owner of a red 545 B.M.W., plate number 832-X9L please head to the parking lot. You are blocking someone in." Millie swiveled around on her barstool and watched as Tia rushed down the steps of the V.I.P. section and head toward the front entrance.

Just as Millie expected, within minutes Omar was out of the V.I.P. section and moving through the crowd. He was only stopping to shake hands and give hugs. Millie began to nibble on her bottom lip as Omar Goodness walked up to the bar. She felt a little slighted when he passed her and headed to where his boy sat accompanied by her two beautiful co-workers. Millie jumped her hot ass up off the stool and walked right over.

"Hello everyone. I-I-I..." Omar stammered as he stared at Joy a little longer than he intended to.

"Omar, this is Joy. Joy this is my good friend Omar," Kinard said with a smile. He seemed overly excited to introduce his friend to the first good moral having woman hat he had met in years.

"Hello Joy," Omar said extending his hand to her and then quickly releasing it. "And who might this be?" Omar asked extending his hand to Bria.

"Oh this is what God sent down to me knowing that she is exactly what I needed in my life. Her name is Bria," Askari answered in a way that only he could say it without it sounding corny.

"Excuse me. I need to go to the ladies room," Joy said grabbing her purse and then hurriedly walking away. Kinard hunched his shoulders.

"Don't mind her. She gets a little nervous when men come around. I think it has something to do with her religion," Millie joked.

Omar's phone vibrated. He read the text message with a look of frustration on his face. "Can y'all give me a second? As a matter of fact, why don't you all meet me back at the V.I.P. in a few minutes," Omar said backing away from the bar.

Millie decided to hit the dance floor. Shaking her ass always made her feel sexy and approachable. Getting Omar's attention was a little more challenging than she expected. Tia returned from the parking lot looking pissed off. She headed to the bar and ordered something strong, a double shot of Remy to be exact. Bria noticed the agitated look on Tia's face and decided to approach her.

"Hey girl. You look like somebody just pissed you off. What's going on?" Bria asked.

"That damn DJ..." Tia said shaking her head. "Talking about my car was blocking somebody in. I get out there and my car was not blocking anybody in. Where's Omar?"

"Oh, he just stepped off. He said he'll be right back," Bria said sizing Tia up. She thought Tia was just beautiful. "Omar is one lucky man and I'm not talking about his riches. I'm talking about your sexy ass. I wish!" Bria said while winking her eyes at Tia. Just then did Tia remember that Millie had informed her that her co-worker Bria went both ways.

"Bria, no disrespect, but I don't get down like that," Tia said trying to be as respectable as possible.

"I respect that. I'm just a greedy bitch. Dick is God's gift to women, but there's no way in the world I could live my life without the sweet taste of a woman or some bomb ass head from a woman. You know a man can never come close to a woman when it comes to eating pussy."

"I don't know about all that, but if you say so," Tia said. She thought about the tongue lashing that Omar had put on her.

"You wouldn't' know, but if you ever wanted to compare, you can just call me. Don't ever hesitate and ummmm, I'll..."

"Bria," Tia exclaimed cutting her off.

"Oh, I'm sorry girl. I got caught up in the moment," Bria said looking Tia up and down one last time and then shaking her head. *"The things I would do to her sexy ass,"* Bria thought to herself and then said, "I heard of this one dude that might be able to keep up though. I'm sure Millie told you about the guy that ripped her homegirl's panties off and then ate her pussy so good that she fainted and had to be taken to the hospital for treatment. I've been looking for him ever since."

Tia was livid on top of being in total shock. She could not believe Millie had the nerve to put her business out in the streets like that, but Tia still had to keep her cool in front of Bria. "Girl you know Millie ass be exaggerating all the damn time. That's my girl and all, but I take her stories with a grain of salt," Tia said.

Askari interrupted their conversation. "Tia do you mind if I take this lovely lady to the dance floor and show her how I get down?"

"Do your thing playa, playa. It's your world," Tia joked and then headed to the dance floor herself. Tia wasn't about to cut a rug though. She was about to cut into Millie's ass who at the time was backing it up on a tall brown skin dude with dreadlocks. "Can I have a word with you," Tia said interrupting their dance by grabbing Millie by her elbow and damn near dragging her off the dance floor.

Party's Over

Joy fixed her makeup inside the lady's room mirror. She had only been in there for three minutes before Omar came busting through the door. He grabbed her by the throat squeezing it a little tighter than he intended slamming her back up against one of the empty stalls.

"What the hell is you doing here, Joy? Huh?" Joy tried to respond, but his grip was too tight so she closed her eyes and slowly licked her lips seductively. Omar knew that one of her guilty pleasures was being choked and man-handled so he let her neck go not wanting to cause her any pleasure at this moment. "Why are you here?" Omar asked through gritted teeth.

"I was invited big daddy, but seeing you all mad like this got my pussy soaking wet. You fucked this pussy so good for wrecking your truck. I could only imagine what you would do to it if I wrecked your party?" Who would have ever thought that Joy, the good girl, the God fearing Christian woman was a rough sex nymphomaniac? Her closest friends even thought she was an undercover nun. I guess it is true what they say about the *good girls*.

"Joy you seriously need some fucking help!"

"What? Sexual extortion is not a crime punishable by the law," Joy said biting her bottom lip and thrusting her crotch into Omar.

"And you would know," Omar said.

"Yup, I looked it up already and even if it was a crime, I'm sure you..." Joy cut her sentence short when she heard voices coming from behind the ladies room door. Someone was about to enter. Omar pulled Joy into an empty stall and locked it with the small latch that was only strong enough to stop a push.

Tia and Millie burst through the door loudly. Without doing a thorough search of the ladies room,

Tia went postal on Millie's ass. "Why the hell did you run your mouth, Millie?"

"Run my mouth... Run my mouth about what?" Millie asked totally caught off guard by Tia's aggressiveness.

"About me and Omar, that's what!"

"Tia you tripping. I never told anyone about you and him and if y'all were trying to be on some down-low type of shit, then why are y'all all lovey dovey up in the V.I.P. for everyone to see?"

"Don't play stupid Millie. You know what I'm talking about."

"Uhhh, actually I don't."

"Well let me spell it out for you. The panty ripping and the hospital. Bria seems to know quite well what she's talking about and who she heard it from."

Okay, but I never told her that Omar was The Panty Ripper and that you was the one who ended up in the damn hospital."

Listening to Tia and Millie's conversation had Joy fuming in the stall with Omar. She reached down and grabbed his balls and squeezed them tightly. Omar doubled over in pain. He wanted to scream bloody murder, but the predicament that he was in only allowed him to contort his face into grimaces which of course made Joy jealous since she was a true freak for pain. She released him just as Tia began to get even more boisterous.

"It don't matter if you said names or not Millie! You promised that you wasn't going to say anything about it, point blank period!!!"

"Well I-I-I," Millie stuttered.

"Well shit!" Tia said cutting Millie's words short. "As a matter of fact, deuces! I'm out," Tia said.

"Tia wait! Where are you going?"

"HOME!" Tia screamed and then barged out of the ladies room with Millie hot on her heels. Omar wanted to chase after her, but it would be very hard for him to explain exactly what he was doing in the bathroom stall with one of Millie's co-workers; the same co-worker that was supposed to be hooking up with his buddy Kinard. Well at least he knew now how Joy found out about him and Tia's panty ripping emergency room experience... Millie!

All the drama seemed to turn Joy on as usual. As soon as she heard the bathroom door close, she immediately dropped down to her knees inside the stall. "Let me suck it big daddy. Let me suck it, please." Omar was disgusted by her antics and downright tired of her bullshit!

"You'll never taste this dick again in your life! If you want to wreck the party, then go right ahead and

right foot on the toilet seat, lifted her dress up, pulled
her panties to the side, and rubbed her clit until she
climaxed all over her fingers.

59

Two Weeks Later

Omar sat in his lavish office in a depressing slump. Tia was not returning any of his calls nor was she responding to his numerous text messages. He hadn't heard anything from her since she walked out, rather stormed out of his party and it was driving him crazy. To make matters worse, Joy was making his life a living hell. She wanted, no she needed Omar to rip her panties off and fuck the sense out of her. Well that is the little bit of sense that she had left. Omar reached inside his cherry wood desk drawer and pulled out the panties that he had slid under the table and strong armed Tia for at the restaurant. He placed them up to his nose and inhaled deeply. They had lost about ninety percent of Tia's scent and Omar was damn near on the verge of tears. His mind started to spin a mile a minute. He had to get Tia back by any means necessary. Omar put the panties on his desk and pulled out his phone. He called his boy Askari. Askari answered on the second ring.

"What's up O," Askari yelled into the receiver excitedly.

"What's good with with you?"

"You know me man. Same old two step with a little twist."

"I hear that, but what's up with Millie's home girl Bria? I know you smashed that by now?" Omar asked.

"I wish! Bria is a little too complex for my patients so I stopped calling her. Why, what's up?"

"I'm trying to get in touch with her home girl Millie," Omar replied without hesitation.

"Well here, take Bria's number. I'm sure she will give you Millie's number," Askari said as he proceeded to give Omar Bria's number. After talking with Omar for a few more minutes, the two gentlemen ended the call. Omar sat at his desk pondering exactly what it was he wanted to say to Millie. She was not one of his most favorite people in the world. In fact, he couldn't stand Millie and her big ass mouth. She was the reason why Tia cut him off and why Joy had wrecked his truck. Omar knew that he had to put his emotions to the side and call Millie. He took a deep breath, exhaled, and then dialed the number.

"Hello," Millie answered on the third ring sounding a little skeptical because of the unfamiliar phone number.

"Hello, can I speak to Millie please?"

"Speaking."

"Hey, what's up? This is Omar, I'm..."

"Omar Goodness?" Millie asked ecstatically.

Omar chuckled, "Yeah the one and only." He knew that Millie had firsthand information about his tongue game which would make any female curious and excited.

"Wowwww! I'm honored. What can I do to you? I mean, for you? What can I do for you, Mr. Goodness?" Millie said correcting herself only to add emphasis to what she originally said. Omar caught it, but let it fly right over his head.

"I was wondering if you heard from Tia lately," he said trying to rain on Millie's parade, but it was him who would need the umbrella when it came to dealing with Millie and her scandalous ways.

"Actually I just got off the phone with her. She's going thru it as usual."

"Going thru it; about what?"

"It's really not my place to say, but her and her ex is back together. They are trying to work thru their differences. They might as well get married because they will never love another, the way they love each other," Millie lied. She hadn't heard from Tia since Omar's party. Omar was devastated. The last thing that he expected to hear was that Tia was back with her ex. That was the same guy that left her so emotionally scarred.

"No wonder she haven't returned any of my calls. All she had to do was let me know," Omar said sounding like a neglected child.

"Omar, Tia has always been and always will be selfish. Giving is not in her DNA. She wouldn't even give you the proper respect and let you know that she's back in a relationship. Now that is sad," Millie said. With friends like Millie's lying ass, one would never need an enemy. "Some people never change," she added sincerely.

OMG

Omar gulped down his double shot of Cognac. This was his third drink and he was feeling good. He already knew that the ringing of his doorbell after midnight could only mean one thing; a booty call. This wasn't just any booty call, this was new pussy. Omar walked to the door wearing nothing but a pair of black Polo boxer briefs which meant that he was *war ready*. He snatched the door open with a vigor that would have int imidated the average chick, but Millie was not your average chick nor did she look like it. When he opened the door, Millie was standing there in Omar's doorway wearing a black Carolina Herrera trench coat, a pair of Valentino shades that concealed her eyes, and a pair of black leather six inch Giuseppe heels. Millie opened her trench coat revealing her almost naked body. She was only wearing a black silk thong under her trench coat.

"I have a special delivery for a Mr. Omar Goodness," Millie said. Omar reached out and snatched her inside the doorway immediately after the words left her mouth.

"Mmph... Mmph... Mmph... Don't be so mean," Millie said seductively. Omar reached behind Millie's back and slammed the door shut. Next he grabbed Millie's hair pulling her head back causing her to look up at the ceiling.

"Imma fuck this pussy until you beg me to stop."

"Ummm," Millie moaned. "Fuck it hard! Break me off a piece of that Kit Kat bar." Millie was a nasty mouth, shit talking super freak, but Omar Goodness had something up his sleeve to shut her mouth up. Millie could already feel her juices starting to flow. Omar marched Millie up the stairs and to his bedroom still holding on to her hair. As they reached the bedroom door, Omar used his other hand to slap Millie on her ass.

"Slow your ass down," Omar said to Millie. She was damn near running. She couldn't wait for Omar to try and make her faint.

Omar kicked his bedroom door open like he was the pussy police and Millie had an outstanding warrant. He roughly pushed her on the bed, snatched off her trench coat, and threw it across the room.

"You think you scaring me? My middle name is *harder*, my last name is *deeper*, and my first name is *faster*," Millie warned still talking trash.

"I got something for that nasty little mouth," Omar threatened.

"If it ain't that dick, then I don't want it," Millie said. She could see Omar's dick bulging through his briefs so she knew her trash talking was having just the effect on him that she wanted.

Omar stepped up onto his bed standing tall, looking down at Millie. She hurriedly scurried up on her knees and began to yank Omar's briefs down to his ankles. He stepped out of them one foot at a time and watched as Millie used both of her hands to take a hold of his throbbing dick. She didn't waste any time taking him in her hot wet mouth. Millie was surgical with the dick. Starting with the head, she licked, slurped, twirled, sucked, and then plopped it out of her mouth for a seductive sound effect. Millie was a beast when it came to dick sucking and she could tell that Omar loved it. She did all of this while staring up at Omar the entire time. She never broke eye contact. After repeating that same method two more times, Millie decided to switch it up on him. She took a good seven inches of his dick in her mouth. It went so far that he was touching the back of her throat. Then she started slowly contracting down on the head for a few seconds and then pulling him out slow to catch her breath. Omar had to grab a hold of her shoulders to brace himself, but Millie wasn't having it. She pushed his hands away still looking up into his eyes.

"Take it like a man," Millie said.

Then she slowly deep throated him again. Then again, and again, and again. Millie knew she had him right where she wanted him. She could feel his dick contracting and his muscles tightening. Millie knew the inevitable was about to happen so she turned it up a notch and sucked Omar's dick in fast forward. Millie was sucking at the speed of lightening until his whole body clenched and he screamed, rather growled, "Aarrrghhhh.... Ahh... Ahh... Ahhhhhh!" Omar shot the biggest load ever down Millie's hungry little throat. He came so hard that he grabbed the bed sheets and curled them up with his toes. Omar's knees buckled causing him to fall down on them. Amazingly Millie bent her upper body downward, but she never lost her grip with her mouth. She literally broke him down like a shotgun and she refused to let go. Omar tried pushing her off of him, but to no avail. The head of his dick was so sensitive that the pleasure was just too much for him to handle, but Millie didn't have any remorse. She wrapped her arms tightly around his waist and literally tried to make his ass faint. She wouldn't give up. She sucked his dick back into an erection. Then and only then did she release him from her mouth with another loud PLOP!

Omar crawled across his king size bed to retrieve a condom from his nightstand. Omar ripped the gold foil from the Magnum packet with the swiftness and tossed it to the side. The beast that roared within Omar would only be satisfied with some hard back breaking sex, so Millie's dreams of getting her pussy fed on was not going to happen that night.

Omar stood up on the bed once again, walked over to where Millie laid waiting, squatted down, and then said, "You and that damn mouth!" Millie thought he was referring to her head game, but Omar was actually talking about the way she messed things up between him and Tia.

"Imma teach," Omar said as he reached down and grabbed a hold of her thong and began to rip it off.

"You a lesson," Omar said trying to finish his sentence. Hearing the fabric ripping had Millie's pussy and ears popping. "About your...," Omar said as Millie felt the last piece of fabric rip and then the silk threads sliding between her soaking wet ass crack. "MOUTH," Omar barked completing his sentence. Then he shoved the pussy juice drenched ripped thong in Millie's mouth. He scooped her up off the bed into the air and guided her legs around his waist, all in one quick motion. Millie could taste her erotic secretion as she moaned with a mouthful of silk.

"Ummmm!" Millie moaned.

Omar grabbed his dick and guided it into her dripping wet twat. He grabbed Millie by the back of her thighs causing her to unhook his waist with her feet. She wrapped her arms around his neck for support and Omar let the upward drilling began. Millie's screams were muffled by her silk thong as Omar wore her ass out. He gave a new meaning to "OMG" and it was "O. Mar. Goodness". Millie had multiple orgasms and just when she thought she couldn't cum again; Omar caused her to have a non-stop sixty second squirt gushing orgasm. Too bad for Millie, Omar was thinking about Tia the whole time. When it was all over, the way Omar left her in the fetal position holding a pillow to her stomach as her body was still being racked by spasms. Millie wouldn't have cared less who he was thinking about because OMG was her only thought.

Lunch Breaking

Millie and Bria sat and ate Caesar salads while Joy patiently waited in the line to place her order. Bria noticed that Millie's greedy ass was only picking at her salad.

"Okay, spill it," Bria said placing her fork down.

"What? Spill what?

"Whatever it is that got you so distracted that you can't even eat your lunch."

Millie sat back in her chair fighting with her inner gossip demon. She couldn't even keep her own secrets.

"Have you ever did something wrong that felt to right that you had to do it again even though you knew you were dead wrong?"

"Hell yeah," Bria said smiling thinking of her first girl on girl experience. "Oh God Millie, what did you do this time? I'm afraid to even ask." Joy walked over just in time to hear Millie's confession.

"Girl I got fucked like an animal and I loved it. I got fucked like the world was about to come to an end," Millie said. Joy wanted to turn around and find another table to eat at. Horny as she was, the last thing she wanted to hear about was sex. It was bad enough that Omar was not returning her calls. Joy shook her head and then sat down.

"Well if the dick was that damn good, then why do you feel so dead wrong about it?" Bria asked and then shoved a fork full of salad into her mouth. Millie dropped her head into her hands trying to formulate the right words to justify her actions, but she couldn't think of anything. After a long pause Millie started to bite her nails and her legs began to shake uncontrollably under the table. The thought alone of how he put the beating on her pussy was making Millie get moist between her legs which caused her words to roll right off of her tongue without thought.

"Because of who it was Bria," Millie said and then took a deep breath. "It was the Panty Ripper; the same guy that made the friend of mine pass out!" Bria covered her mouth in shock.

"YOU BITCH!!!" Joy screamed jumping to her feet and storming out of the diner. Bria sat there with her hand still covering her mouth in shock of Millie's confession and Joys reaction to it. That was the first time either of them ever heard Joy swear and both Millie and Bria burst out laughing. They laughed for a good two minutes straight.

"Let me go find this girl before she come back in here throwing Holy water on you," Bria joked and then left in search of Joy.

Joy was not hard to locate. She stood right outside the diner pressing a text message into her phone to God knows who. "Joy! Girl, what in the world is you so upset about?" Bria asked.

"You wouldn't understand," Joy said flatly.

"Try me."

"Men are such idiots."

"Bria laughed and said, "Yes they are. I could have told you that a long time ago, so you're not mad at Millie for sleeping with her friends man?"

"The Panty Ripper is not Tia's man," Joy slipped.

"Tia?" Bria asked dumbfounded.

"Yeah Tia, Millie's friend. That's who Millie stabbed in the back. After Tia told her that Omar made her pass out from the oral sex he gave her," Joy said slipping again. At this point, she was just caught up in the moment and her emotions were taking over.

"OMAR!" Bria screamed in surprise.

"Yes Omar Goodess, The Panty Ripper! Everyone knows but you," Joy said.

"Wait a minute! Wait a minute! Wait a damn minute," Bria said trying to take everything in and process it at the same time. "Well how the hell did you know and I didn't?

"BECAUSE OMAR GOODESS, THE PANTY RIPPER OR WHATEVER YOU WANT TO CALL HIM IS MY GODDAMN MAN," Joy screamed.

Bria's mouth fell wide open and so did Millie's who had just walked out of the diner and into the biggest bombshell of her life.

Not Many Of Us Have Them... Friends

Tia sat alone at the bar drinking Peach Ciroc. It had been two weeks since she ran into Joy at the mall. When she saw Joy at the mall, Joy caused a big scene telling Tia to stay away from *her* man. Tia was extremely embarrassed as Joy screamed, "God don't like ugly and that's why you fainted when my man ate your pussy! You fucking amateur! I taught him that and after lots of practice might I add. And maybe if you would have kept your big mouth closed, your best friend Millie wouldn't have snuck behind your back and fucked my man too!" Tia ran out the mall embarrassed with tears streaming down her face.

Tia shook her head. The thought of Millie's sneaky disloyal ass disgusted her. Tia threw back the sweet tasting Ciroc and told the bartender to fill her back up. She was already on the fifth drink, but who was counting.

"Hey stranger," Tia heard a voice say coming from her left. She turned to see who was greeting her and saw that it was Bria, Millie's friend of all people.

"Hey," Tia responded with absolutely no indication that she wanted the conversation to go any further than that.

"You know this is the second time we bumped into each other at a bar," Bria said trying to strike up a conversation. Tia hunched her shoulders as if to say, *who give a shit!* Bria ordered two shots of Patron and threw them back like a pro and then she immediately ordered two more. She raised her next drink up in front of her and then said, "men, we don't need em anyway."

Bria tossed the shot back and then slammed the glass down on the bar top. "Friends neither!"

"Now I'll drink to that! Salute," Tia said slurring a little and then she gulped down the rest of her drink.

One hour and ten drinks later, Bria was leading Tia into her apartment by her hands. Bria locked the door behind them and walked Tia to her bedroom. Tia began to sober up as Bria walked around the room lighting lavender scented candles. Next Bria turned on some slow music and Tia could not help but to feel catered to in a way that she had never felt before.

Bria was extremely feminine on the outside which helped Tia's mind be a little at ease. Tia never thought in a million years that she could feel so turned on by another woman, but here she was about to engage in something that she had never thought of in her entire life. She had absolutely no idea what to do first and Bria had already sensed that.

"Just lie back on the bed, beautiful and let me handle the rest," Bria said in a voice so sweet that Tia's nipples stood at attention. Tia lay back on the bed as she was instructed to do and Bria did not waste any time getting her out of her dress. The blue Victoria Secret's angel wing panties that Tia wore had her pussy looking like a fluffy blueberry muffin. Bria's mouth began to water at the sight. She slowly crawled between Tia's legs. The anticipation was driving Tia wild. Bria pushed Tia's left leg up causing her left foot to be planted flat on the bed.

"No man will ever make you feel like this," Bria whispered seductively between Tia's legs causing her to squirm. "Not even Omar Goodness," Bria said. Tia almost creamed herself as she lifted her head off the bed to watch Bria in action and that's when Bria did the unimaginable. Using only her teeth, Bria began ripping Tia's panties off, piece by piece.... by.... piece...

Bria the Diva vs. Omar Goodness

Tia Fields walked inside of Neiman Marcus to do a little shopping. She was having dinner tonight with the love of her life at a five star restaurant so she wanted to make sure that she looked flawless from head to toe. Tia picked out a red backless Christian Dior dress that she had her eye on all week.

She stepped in and out of the fitting room in less than two minutes. The red Dior dress was fitting as if it was painted on her body. Tia did a full 360 in the full length mirror outside of the dressing room to check out the most important part of the dress which was her ass area.

"*Perfect*," she said to out loud to herself clearly pleased with what she saw.

"Perfect is an understatement," a voice said from behind her. Tia spun around quickly, a little startled by the closeness of the voice. When she turned around, there he stood looking as handsome and sexy as ever, but she would never complement his no-good ass.

"Didn't your mother ever teach you that it's rude to sneak up on people," Tia said trying to control the butterflies that were fluttering around in her stomach.

"I'm sorry, let me try this again. Hello Ms. Tia Fields, good to see you."

"Hello Mr. Omar Goodness, wish I could say the same," Tia said walking back inside the dressing room to quickly change. After she changed back into her clothes, she exited the dressing room and Omar was still there as she knew he would be. "So how's Millie," Tia asked sarcastically as she walked to the cashier.

"You would know better than me. After I found out that she lied about you and your ex being back together, I never spoke to her again, and I never will," Omar said with a little attitude in his voice.

"Well even if it was true, which it wasn't; does that give you the right to fuck my best friend? Uhhh no!" Tia stopped to look at a Chanel dress.

"You absolutely right. I got played and I played myself, but I want you to know that I will never trust or love another woman again in my life until you come back to me Tia," Omar said in all honesty.

Tia lifted up her left hand showing Omar her engagement ring. "It's a little too late Omar, but here's what I suggest. Do not go through life avoiding love because it's a beautiful thing. Take care of yourself Omar. I have to go."

Bria the Diva

B rianna Jones, better known as Bria the Diva sat
in the V.I.P. Section of the most popular lesbian
club in town. She was hands down the center of
attention wearing a silver ass hugging B.C.B.G. mini-
skirt that did not leave much to the imagination. The
black leather six inch Christian Louboutins made her
ass poke out like a Station Wagon and her confidence
shoot to the roof.

They all wanted Bria, the lesbians, the dykes, the
fems, the bi-sexuals, and even the bi-curious. Not only

was she the baddest bitch in the club in heels, but rumor had it that Bria had the best tongue game in America. That just made her even more desirable. It was a well-known fact that Bria had a wifey so if you were lucky enough to be one of her jump-offs, then you should feel honored and just know your place and enjoy the ride.

"What's up superstar," one of Bria's jump-offs said walking up to her.

"Hey beautiful, long time no see," Bria replied with a smile. The last time Bria saw Sugar, they were in a hotel room. Bria had sucked on her pussy so good that Sugar fell off of the bed trying to get away from her and gushed a puddle on the rug.

Bria stood up to give Sugar a hug. "You better learn how to answer that damn phone when you see me calling," Sugar said leaning into the hug and whispering in her ear.

"Damn you smell good," Bria confessed.

"Taste even better," Sugar said and then walked away with a sexy strut while still looking back at Bria over her shoulders.

"Bria the diva, what's up bitch?" Bria's side kick Apple screamed with her ratchet ass.

"Ay girl. Where ya loud ass coming from?"

"From the snack bar. You know a bitch don't play no games when it comes to food. Bitches in here trying to act cute like they ass ain't hungry. Hummp! Not me," Apple said with absolutely no shame in her game.

"Guess who's in here?"

"WHO?" Apple screamed sounding very ratchet.

"Kilo," Bria replied with a giggle.

"Please, ain't nobody thinking about Kilo broke ass. Always trying to get somebody to suck on that little funky ass strap-on. Ugh!"

Bria burst out laughing until her phone began to vibrate. She contemplated hitting the ignore button, but quickly changed her mind.

"Hey baby," Bria said into the phone. It was wifey.

"I miss you."

"I miss you too my love," was Bria's reply.

"Then come home now."

"Alright, I will be there in a few," Bria said into the phone.

"What's a few?"

"I don't know. I..."

"I don't have on anything, but a blindfold," she said cutting Bria off.

"I'm leaving right now," Bria said and just like that, Bria was out.

Making It Rain

Bria walked in the house and went straight to her bedroom to find her wifey. When she walked into the bedroom, she found her wifey, Tia Fields laying, rather squirming under the sheets. Bria immediately peeled herself out of the B.C.B.G. skirt.

"I see you started without me."

"Ummm... Hmmmm...," was Tia's only reply.

"I'll be back in a few. Let me go freshen up a little, beautiful."

"Hurry up baby. I need to ummm, taste you."

Bria was in and out of the shower in no time. When she stepped back into her bedroom, Tia was still under the sheets. Bria could hear the buzzing from Tia's favorite toy which was a pink pocket rocket. Bria knew that Tia was only teasing herself. She would always bring herself close to an orgasm and then stop and wait for Bria to come home and send her to the moon.

"You need some help with that?" Bria asked seductively as eh pulled the sheet off of Tia. When Bria pulled the sheet back, Tia laid there with her mint green Jimmy Choo pumps on, a mint green thong, and nothing else. Bria crawled on the bed and in between Tia's legs. She pulled Tia's hand out of her thong which still held the pocket rocket. Bria took the pocket rocket, turned it off, and then stuck it in her mouth. She seductively sucked all of Tia's juices off of the toy. "Ummm... ummm... ummm...," Bria moaned in delight. "Why are you laying here with that thong on baby?" Bria asked.

Tia ran her hands through her hair swaying her head from side to side on the pillow. "So you could rip them off."

"That's what you want?" Bria asked as she laid flat on her stomach to get the proper angle between Tia's legs.

"Yes baby!"

"What else you want? Tell me," Bria asked as she began to kiss Tia's inner thighs.

"I want you to make this pussy cum baby," Tia said

"Ummm, what else?"

"I want you to sit on my face. Ummm, and cum all in my mouth." Tia couldn't get another word out as Bria began to pull at her thong with her teeth. Tia heard the first bit of fabric began to rip and she screamed out loud, "YESSSS BABY! JUST LIKE THAT!"

After a minute of tugging, biting, and panty ripping, Tia's thong was no longer attached to her body. It was now in Bria's hand. Bria had a few tricks of her own that drove Tia and the rest of the women she had been with wild. Using the ripped thong, Bria tied Tia's ankles together and then bent Tia's legs back to where her knees were damn near sitting on her perky breast.

"Now hold on right here," Bria instructed. Tia reached up with both hands grabbing a hold of the ripped thong that bound her ankles together. Bria could see the juices threatening to run out of Tia's clean shaven pussy. Tia was extremely wet. Bria reached out and slowly slid her middle finger in Tia's pussy and pulled it out. The juices that were threatening to run out started to slowly trickle down making its way to Tia's asshole, but Bria intercepted them with her lips sucking it like she was sipping on some hot coco. Tia's whole body tensed at the sound and feeling of it which caused Bria to make a nose dive face first into Tia's pussy.

"OH MY GOD!!!" Tia screamed as Bria sucked and teased her clit. Then Bria jabbed her tongue in and out of her love hole. "OHHH BABY! I LOVE YOU SO FUCKING MUCH! OH YES BABY! RIGHT THERE! RIGHT FUCKING THERE!" Tia screamed as she felt the roller-coaster build up inside her body. "Don't stop Bria! Please don't stop." Bria had no intention on stopping as she continued to suck and slurp all over Tia's pussy. "Ohhh! Ohhhhh, here it comes baby! Here it... OHHH I'M CUMING!!! Ahhh... Ah... Ahhh... Ahhhhhhhhh..."

"Ummm (slurp), ummm (slurp)," Bria was getting every last drop of it and just as Tia's body began to shake like she just got shocked by a Taser, Bria began to sip on her overflowing juices. It sounded like Bria was sipping soup out of a bowl and she was only getting started. She jammed two fingers inside of Tia, curled her fingers up toward her G-spot, and started to make the come here gesture with her fingers.   drove Tia wild until she could no longer hold her legs up in that position and they fell on Bria's back.

"Oh baby, what are you doing to me," Tia cried out.

Bria lifted her soaking wet face. "I'm just claiming what's mine." Bria dipped her head back low and continue to suck on Tia's clit while she massaged her G-spot with her two fingers.

"It's yours baby! Ummm... Oh it's... Ohhh shit! Oh fuck! Suck this pussy baby! Suck it baby! Suck it reallllll good! I'm bout to squirt baby! I'm bout to squirt! Arrggggh!" And that's exactly what she did. Tia squirted right inside of Bria's hungry mouth and all over her face. Tia laid her head back on the pillow totally spent with her pussy still jumping. She felt Bria moving around, but she didn't have the energy to lift her head up again. Then she heard a familiar buzzing sound. It was the buzzing of the pocket rocket. Tia tried to crawl away from it, but Bria grabbed her and pulled her back to the middle of the bed. "Don't you do it! Don't you run from me," Bria said with a sinister smiler on her face.

Distraction

Tia Fields sat at her desk swamped in paperwork. Her computer was taking forever to boot up and her boss was being a jerk as usual. Working as a paralegal in a struggling law firm was not her dream job, but it paid the bills so she tried to make the best of it.

There was a knock at her office door. As bad as her morning was already going, the last thing she wanted to see was the delivery man holding flowers in his hands when she opened the door.

"Sign her please," the delivery man said quickly as if his morning was going just as bad as Tia's.

"Thank you," she said and then closed the door. Tia already knew who the flowers were from so she took the card out, walked over to her waste basket, and dropped them in it. Now back at her desk, Tia raked her fingers through her hair in frustration. Then she picked up the card that came with the flowers, opened it, and read the message out loud.

To: My Moon,

Let's make a trade

I'll give you my life

In exchange for your heart

I'll sign over everything I own

In exchange for your heart, because

To have everything except love

Is to have nothing at all...

Omar Goodness

"*Damn*," Tia said to herself knowing Omar was a successful millionaire. He did make her faint from his tongue game. Tia looked around her small unorganized office and thought, "*I could quit right now.*" Then she thought of Bria who she loved with all of her heart. Then she read Omar's card again and then she thought about Bria again. Then she thought about Omar and

Millie which would always be a deal breaker. Tia balled up the card in her hand and tossed it in the waste basket with the flowers.

Tia's lunch break couldn't have come any quicker. She rushed out of the office building like it was on fire. As soon as she got outside and started to breathe the fresh air, she started to relax. Just as she started to relax, she looked up and saw no one other than Omar Goodness who was standing there leaned up against a white Bently GT.

"Did you get the flowers that I sent you and the card that came along with them?"

"Why are you standing outside of my job, Omar?"

"I was in the neighborhood."

Tia walked right pass him. "Would love to chat," she lied. "But, I only have an hour break." Omar rose up off the car and was hot on her heels.

"Can I buy you lunch?"

"No thank you," she replied.

"Well, can I eat with you? I'm starving."

"It's a free country. You can eat wherever you please." As soon as the words came out of her mouth, she regretted them. Tia looked over at Omar who had the silliest smile on his face and even she had to laugh. "You know what I mean Omar," Tia said shaking her head trying to hide the fact that she was blushing.

Omar held the door for her as they entered the Chinese buffet.

Twenty minutes later Omar was all smiles as they ate. "I don't know why you sitting over there looking so happy because this is not a date," Tia reminded him.

"Okay, okay, okay, but can I ask you a personal question?"

"I'm listening," Tia said and then shove some Lo Mein into her mouth.

"Who's the lucky guy that put the ring on your finger?"

"That, I will not discuss with you," Tia said.

"Okay cool. Did y'all set a date yet?"

"We are not talking about this Omar," Tia said shoving more food into her mouth.

"What if I wanted to send a gift?"

Tia pointed her fork at Omar. "Don't go there."

"Well can I at least jump out of the cake at your bachelorette party? I will get all oiled up and I will only wear a pair of cowboy boots," Omar said. Tia burst out laughing.

"You know I love it when you do that right," Omar said seriously.

"Do what?"

"Smile."

"Well I hated when you made me cry," Tia confessed.

"And I'm sorry for that. Until I take my last breath Tia, I will be waiting for you. Just promise me if things don't work out in your marriage... I don't care if its twenty years from now, just promise me that you will give me one more chance." Tia was touched and she could see in Omar's eyes that he really loved her.

"Omar, twenty years from now, you'll probably be happily married with five kids."

Omar grabbed Tia's hand and then whispered in her ear, "I'll never be truly happy unless I'm with you Ms. Tia Fields." Tia saw the water well up in his eyes and her first instinct was to get up and hug him. This was even surprising for herself, but what most surprising is that she wanted to love him.

On a Mission

Omar Goodness was driving himself crazy trying to find out who Tia was engaged to. He did everything except hire a private investigator and that's only because it never crossed his mind. The one person he was sure of, that had to know who he really was... Was Millie! Even though neither he nor Tia had spoken to her in over a year. Omar was sure that the queen of gossip still wore her crown. He didn't know if Millie still worked at her same job, but he could find out real easy from Joy. Sure it was going to cost him some dick and whatever freaky shit Joy wanted him to do to her, but if it was his only option, then so be it. The crazy things people would do for love, and there was no exception when it came to Omar Goodness, The Panty Ripper.

En-Joy

After stopping at the local drugstore to pick up a few items he went straight to Joy's house to turn her freaky ass out. Omar was ringing her doorbell non-stop. Joy looked through the peephole and almost had a panic attack. She unlocked the door with shaky hands and opened the door.

"What took you so long?" Omar said in an aggressive tone.

"I'm sorry big daddy. I wasn't expecting you," Joy replied in a submissive tone. Omar stepped in the house slamming the door behind him which made Joy's heart skip a beat and her pussy start to pulsate. He noticed that she was wearing her workout attire, a wife beater, a pair of spandex pants, and a pair of Nike running sneakers.

"Get over here," Omar demanded pointing to the floor right in front of his feet.

"Big daddy, can I freshen up? I'm all sweaty."

"GET YOUR ASS OVER HERE NOW!" Omar screamed.

"NO," Joy screamed back and then ran up the stairs knowing that would enrage Omar and make him bust her pussy wide open. Omar gave chase and caught up with her at the top of the stairs pulling her back down. Joy's knees were on the third step to the top while her hands rested flat on the second floor landing. Omar reached out and yanked her spandex down pass her ass. The first thing that he noticed was that she didn't have any panties on that he could rip off and that caused him to smack her on the ass rather hard causing a stinging sensation.

"Toot that ass up," Omar demanded and without hesitation Joy complied. Omar immediately pulled his pants down to his knees and then he retrieved the little bag of items he had purchased at the drugstore. He opened the box of Magnums and quickly slid one on. Next he pulled out a small bottle of KY Jelly. Joy looked back and when she saw the bottle in Omar's hands, she tried to hurry to her feet, but Omar stung her on the ass again with another hard slap. "Don't move! Now toot that ass back up for daddy!" Joy did as she was told and Omar began to squirt KY Jelly all down the crack of her ass. Using one of his fingers, he plunged it into her asshole. While his finger was still in her ass, he began to squirt more KY Jelly around his finger and then he gently shoved another finger in her ass.

"Ohhhh big daddy lube that asshole up and then fuck it until I scream! You going to make me scream big daddy? Huh?"

Omar responded by taking his two fingers out of Joy's ass and slowly and gently sliding his brick hard dick into it, all the way to his balls. Joy started to scream out in pure ecstasy. "Oh it hurt so good big daddy!" After only a few long deep strokes, Omar lost his mind inside of her tight little asshole.

About five minutes of pounding was all Omar could give before he grunted and then shot a knee buckling load into Joy's ass. Joy crawled her way to the bathroom with a gaping asshole and turned the shower on. As soon as the water got hot, she hopped right in.

The hot shower was exactly what she needed. She had only been in the shower for about a minute and in walked Omar with a cocky grin on his face. He opened the shower door and walked right in.

"Wash me," was all Omar said and Joy was more than happy to oblige. She dropped to her knees and washed his dick as if it was her most prized possession.

"I'm sorry big daddy," she said looking up at him.

"Sorry for what?"

"For not having any panties on for you to rip off," Joy said.

"Just don't let it happen again."

After the shower, it was time for some pillow talk. That was Omar's main reason for being there. "So how's work," he asked, but not really caring.

"Work is work, you know. I rush to get there and then I can't wait to leave."

"I hear that. Do you still work with your two friends, Bria and Millie?"

"Bria quit, but Millie still works there. Do you want me to tell her you miss her?" Joy asked with a twinge of an attitude. "Everybody knows that she tattooed O.M.G. on her ass in big black bold letters, stupid ho!" Omar laughed to himself thinking back to the night when he ripped Millie's panties off and saw that tattoo for the first time. He couldn't help, but to think about how he wore that ass out that night

Brown Sugar

Bria and Apple sat close to the stage making it rain on a stripper named Skittles who had a tattoo of a rainbow on her back. Skittles was controlling the stage and working the pole as if that was what she was born to do.

"Can I taste the rainbow?" Apple asked with a smile as she stuffed a few bills inside Skittles' thong. Bria was trying to be on her best behavior since her boo Sugar danced at the same club and was probably somewhere close by watching her like a hawk.

"YEAH I LOVE THE STIPPERS! YEAH I LOVE THE STRIPPERS," Apple sang along with the 2 Chains song that rocked through the speakers in the club. Bria stood up and started to dance while she tossed dollar bills on a stripper that had more ass than a donkey. Suddenly she felt two hands wrap around her waist from behind. She looked over her shoulder and saw that it was Sugar.

"Hey sexy. What's your name?" Sugar asked playfully.

"Kitten," Bria said playing along.

"Well if that's the case. I taut I taw a puddy tat," Sugar said in her best Tweety Bird voice.

"You did! You did! You did see a puddy cat," Bria said and they both burst out laughing at their Tweety Bird and Sylvester impersonations. Then Sugar grabbed Bria's hand and lead her to the champagne room for a private show. Sugar sat Bria down and then quickly straddled her. Bria was like a drug, she seemed to make most women horny. Real drugs like Molly and Ecstasy didn't have shit on Bria. Sugar gently kissed her on the lips before she spoke.

"I need to taste you baby. It's been so long," Sugar said while grinding her pussy into Bria's lap.

"I'm going to call you as soon as I can get free," Bria promised.

"You free now. Let's get a room," Sugar said. "Ummmm," she moaned in Bria's ear and then stuck her tongue in it. Sugar was on fire and Bria felt bad that she couldn't leave with her. Tia had already made her promise not to stay out too late.

"I can't sweetness," Bria said as she slid Sugar's thong to the side and began to massage her clit with two fingers. "Just give me some time beautiful and I promise, I'm going to suck this pussy to sleep."

"Ohhh... Ohhh... Okay... You gon make me cum," Sugar said moaning and she started to grind her hips harder against Bria's fingers.

"How did you get this wet, sexy?"

"You made me this wet... mmm...mmm...mmm..."

"Who sugar water is this," Bria asked and then popped one of Sugar's titties out and started to lick and suck on it.

"Ummmm... Hmmmm...."

"Right now! Can I cum right now? Ohhhh, I'm cumming! OHHHHHH! OH! OOOHHHHH!" Sugar's body began to shudder along with her words as she gushed all over Bria's fingers. Bria stuck two fingers inside of Sugar's pussy, making sure she coated her fingers up real good with Sugar's juices and then she pulled them out and stuck them in Sugar's mouth. Sugar didn't hesitate to suck the cum off of Bria's fingers. Then Bria's phone began to ring. Call it a woman's intuition because it was none other than Tia calling and that meant it was time for Bria to go.

Making Amends

Omar sat slumped back in a rental car outside of Joy's job. He watched as she exited the building, got in her car, and headed home. No more than five minutes later, Millie exited the same building looking fine as hell, but Omar saw her as the devil in sheep's clothing. To him, Millie was the true definition of a *shady bitch* so he knew that he had to be extremely careful with what he was planning on doing.

Omar pulled the rental car close to the curb where Millie strutted along and beeped the horn. Millie had to do a double-take. At first she thought her eyes were playing tricks on her so she pulled down her Roberto Cavalli shades and yup it was him, Mr. OMG in the flesh.

"Get in. I need to talk to you," Omar said out the window.

"Get in? Nahhhh, I seen this movie 100 times and I already know how it ends," Millie said.

"I don't know what you talking about," Omar said.

"I know you still hate me Omar. I haven't seen you in about a year and now out of the blue you come to pick me up at my job so you can take me somewhere, cut me up into little pieces, and then the authorities will never find my body," Millie said while laughing, but she was dead serious. It had been a while, but Millie still had her personality. Some things never changed.

Omar laughed and said, "You watch way too much T.V. Okay, I'll get out then." Omar pulled right behind Millie's X5 and got out and showed Millie his hands. "See, no knife," he said shaking his head.

Millie chuckled lightly. "So this is an awkward surprise. What's going on Omar?"

Omar thought about beating around the bush, but then decided against it. "Did you hear anything about Tia getting married?"

"Oh so this is what this is all about? Tia... I should have known," Millie said sucking her teeth.

"Yeah you should have. It probably would have been us getting married if it wasn't for your lying selfish ass," Omar snapped.

Millie smiled, "Damn! You still pussy whipped over some pussy that you never got!"

"It's not about sex with everybody. Haven't you ever heard of---," Omar said cutting his sentence short. He quickly caught himself, but apparently not quickly enough.

"Of what? Love of course. I've heard of love and I'm sure Tia's in love and that's why she's getting married," Millie said matter-of-factly. Millie's comment hit Omar like a ton of bricks. All he could do was slump his shoulders.

"I need your help Millie," Omar said in a pleading tone of voice.

"My help?" Millie asked totally confused.

"Yeah, I need you to help me get her back."

"And how the hell am I supposed to do that? You know Tia hates my guts."

"I don't know. Think of something, please. You was very creative when it came to separating us."

"But Omar, I don't even know who she is marrying," Millie confessed.

"Well find out and then help me stop it from happening."

"Don't you think that we put her through enough already," Millie said making a good point, but Omar wasn't hearing it. He felt that he had to get Tia back and by any means necessary.

"I love her Millie and I need to get her back, bottom line."

Millie twirled her hair around her fingers as if she was in deep thought and then said, "Okay, let's say I do this for you. What's in it for me?"

"What do you want? Just name it and it's yours," Omar promised.

"What do I want?" Millie asked seductively. "Do you really need to ask Mr. Omar Goodness? I want my panties ripped off and I want to be fucked like your life depends on it! I want you to eat this pussy like it's your last dinner, bottom line!"

WZ200 Radio

This is your morning show at WZ200. I am your host Izzy Al and if you're still in bed... WAKE YOU ASS UP! WAKE YO ASS UP!" Tia was on her way to work, but there was no way she was going to miss the morning show, not this morning anyway. "We have a special guest in the studio with us today. The man that's in charge of our women bringing sexy back to the bedroom, the one and only Mr. Omar Goodness."

"Izzy Al, good morning," Omar said. *"Listen at his sexy ass voice,"* Tia thought to herself.

"Yes it is a good morning. The phone lines are already lighting up. So let's talk about this new design that you put out that got the whole damn world buzzing."

"Well when I started the panty line Goodies, I set out to be the biggest distributer that this market has ever seen with affordable, but still sexy under garments. I exceeded those expectations overnight so now I just want to make sure that I keep things spicy for the consumers," Omar explained.

"And that you did with your new line of candy scented ladies underwear," Izzy Al agreed thinking about his own personal experience.

"I'm a firm believer that any kind of Goodies should look good, taste good, and last but not least, smell good," Omar stated.

Tia caught herself zoning out to Omar's voice. Without even realizing it, she had placed her hand between her upper thighs close to her Goodies and began to squeeze them together tightly as she listened to Omar talk about his newest venture.

"To answer a lot of women's concerns about the candy scented underwear, I can assure you that no chemical was used that will cause any type of yeast infections, urinary tract infections, or any other vaginal infections for that matter."

"Well Mr. Omar Goodness, we got a Lisa on line one that would like to have a word with you. Lisa go ahead and speak. You are on the line with Omar Goodness," Izzy Al said and then pushed a button to connect the caller.

"Oh my God! Good morning Mr. Goodness," Lisa said.

"Good morning Lisa. You can call me Omar if you like."

"Nahhh, I like Mr. Goodness. It sounds much sexier." Tia rolled her eyes at the caller through her car radio.

"Okay, if you like it, I love it. What's your question or comment Lisa?"

"Well I just want to personally thank you for putting out the candy scented panties. My man never liked taking a trip down town, but ever since I started wearing your scented panties, it's like he rented an apartment down there."

For the next half hour Tia listened to caller after caller praise Omar Goodness. She wanted to go down to the radio station and congratulate him in person, but decided not to. What she wanted even more was to forgive him and then make sweet love to him. "After he rips my panties off," she thought to herself. Tia dropped her head inside of her hands. She promised herself not to ever let Omar Goodness occupy not even a tiny bit of space in her head ever again. That was easier said than done because there he was occupying her every thought.

Drama

Bria was in the shower when her phone began to ring. This was the fourth call back to back that rung all the way out which made Tia feel that it might be some type of family emergency. Normally Tia wouldn't answer Bria's phone, but something about the four consecutive calls told her to answer it; especially when she looked at the phone and saw that the number that was calling Bria was blocked. Tia pressed the talk button and didn't get the chance to say hello before the female's voice on the other end exploded with emotion.

"Why are you doing this to me, Bria? Do you expect me to just sit on the sideline and ignore how I feel about you? Why don't you ever answer your phone and why the hell do I---"

Tia cut the caller off. "Excuse me?" Tia asked. "Who is this?" Once the caller realized that it was not Bria on the other line, she panicked.

"Oh, I'm sorry. Wrong number!" (CLICK) The call was disconnected.

"Wrong number my ass," Tia mumbled and then stormed into the bathroom snatching back the shower curtain catching Bria by surprise. "You fucking around on me?" Tia asked as she held Bria's phone up.

"What?"

"You heard what the fuck I said!"

"Baby, why are you cursing at me?" Bria asked.

"Brianna, you better answer my question!"

"No, I would never," Bria lied with a straight face knowing that the truth was too ugly.

"So who the hell is this bitch calling your phone talking about she's sitting on the sideline?"

"You answered my phone?"

"What phone? This phone?" Tia asked and then politely dropped Bria's phone inside the toilet. Bria was speechless as she quickly stepped out of the shower and wrapped her body with a towel. Then she fished her phone out of the toilet bowl and lucky for her, the new IPhone was water proof.

"Tia, you tripping!"

"Well until you figure out how to properly and honestly answer my questions, I'll be tripping alone! Get dressed and leave and if you messed around with that bitch that called your phone, do all three of us a favor and don't come back!"

Apple's

B ria sat still in Apples' apartment looking very uncomfortable. "Bria don't be sitting over there acting cute like you never seen no damn roaches before."

"Not this damn many," Bria said to herself. "Girl, I'm not thinking about no damn roaches right now."

"Oh cause homeless people can't be choicy," Apple joked. "You want some Kool-Aid?"

"Hell to the no," Bria said to herself. "No thank you, I'm okay."

"Bitch you don't know what you missing. This shit here is the bomb! I mix like six different flavors together," Apple said and then came and sat right across from Bria in her living room. "So who do you think that it was that called?"

"Who the hell knows. What Tia don't realize is that a lot of these people had my number before me and her became serious."

"If that's your story then stick to it," Apple said and then gulped down every last bit of the Kool-Aid that she had poured in the Mayo jar. Apple let out the loudest burp that Bria had ever heard before.

"Eeewwww! That was real lady like, Apple," Bria said. Apple was ghetto with a capital G, but she was still Bria's homegirl. Her and Bria had been friends since grade school and nothing was going to change that. Not once did they ever come close to being intimate. Minus the fact that Apple was the definition of ratchet, she was still a very attractive young lady with an ass that could swallow up a G-string. Some people even said that she resembled Megan Good with her high cheek bones and her succulent lips.

"Oh that's my song," Apple said jumping up off the couch. She dug her funky looking sweatpants out of the crack of her butt and then turned the radio all the way up and sung along with the song. "Two bad

bitches at the same damn time, at the same damn time."
And just when Bria thought that things couldn't have
gotten any rowdier, Kilo walked through the door
without even knocking with two other manly looking
chicks. Kilo and the chick with the hairs on her chin
sandwiched Apple in the middle of the floor dancing
and singing right along with her. "At the same damn
time, at the same damn time." The third one walked up
to Bria and tried to hand her a 40 ounce of Malt Liquor,
"You drinking, Ma?"

"No, no thank you," Bria said excusing herself and
went into the bedroom to call Sugar.

"Hey, what's up sweetness?"

"Not a damn thing when you're not around," Sugar
replied.

"Did you call my phone earlier?" Bria asked.

"No. Why?"

"Tia answered my phone and all hell broke loose,"
Bria said.

"Are you alright?"

"Not really. I had a sour day and I could really use
something sweet right about now," Bria said in a sexy
tone of voice.

"Well, what's sweeter than Sugar baby?"

"Nothing at all! I'm on my way," Bria said and then
ended the call. One of Bria's curls fell from the side of

her head and landed on her ear. Bria thought it was a roach and freaked the fuck out! She ran out of the bedroom full speed smacking her ear and shaking her collar out. She was screaming, "GET IT OFF OF ME! GET IT OFF OF ME!" Apple and her company looked at Bria like she was crazy as she ran right out of Apples' roach infested apartment still screaming.

"No this bitch didn't," Apple said feeling a little embarrassed. "I'mma curse her motherfucking ass out as soon as I see her!"

Millie's on the Move

Millie was working her magic as she sat and got a pedicure in the same shop that she and Tia had come to together for years. Ms. Lee was just as bad as her customers when it came to the latest gossip. For an old Chinese lady, her ass was always on point with it.

"I see whoever has been doing your feet, do not do good job," Ms. Lee said as she worked on Millie's toes.

"I miss you too Ms. Lee. I know you are the best. I moved to the other side of town so it's kind of difficult to commute."

"Hmp! They say you lay down with friend boyfriend. Tell me not true."

"That was not her boyfriend. They never even, how you put it, lay down together, but I was still wrong for what I did."

"Well still not bad like what she do. In my country, no, no, very forbidden," Ms. Lee explained.

"What? What she do Ms. Lee? I haven't seen her in a very long time," Millie said.

"What she do? She lay down with woman."

"YOU LIE!!!" Millie screamed and then covered her mouth with her hand in shock.

"I no lie! They come here together twice a month."

"For how long? How long have they been together?"

"Ohhh, I say ten months now," Ms. Lee said.

"When the next time they be here?" Millie asked.

"Next week, Friday at 4 o'clock. Why? You come make peace with friend?"

"I don't know, but don't tell her you seen me. Okay?"

"Okay," Ms. Lee said unconvincingly.

"Okay Ms. Lee?" Millie had to drive it home with Ms. Lee and her loose lips.

"I say okay! Me no say nothing!"

Friday

Friday couldn't have gotten here any quicker for Millie's impatient ass. If Ms. Lee's accusations were correct, which they usually were, then boy did she have a story to tell Omar. Millie silently prayed that it was true even though if she had to bet on it, she wouldn't put her money on it. She had known Tia Fields for a very long time and one thing she was not and that was a carpet muncher.

Millie sat in the parking lot no more than twenty minutes before Tia's read 545 B.M.W. pulled into the lot. Millie didn't realize how much she missed Tia until she saw her car pull up. The driver's door swung open and so did the passenger's door. Millie was breaking her neck to see if Tia really had a girlfriend. The driver stepped out and to Millie's surprise it was not Tia, it was Bria. Then Tia stepped out of the passenger side and the two of them walked inside the shop hand in hand. A bug could have flew inside of Millie's mouth because it was stuck wide the hell open. *"Tia and Brianna,"* she thought to herself shaking her head in disbelief. Her next thought was even more mind blowing, *"marriage."* Millie was not sure if this would be good or bad news for Omar, but he was definitely going to have to pay for this information. She knew enough about Bria to write a book, which would make it that much easier to throw shade over her and Tia's relationship.

Goodies Incorporated

"**W**HAT!?!" Omar screamed jumping out of his seat. He damn near knocked everything off of his desk.

"I kid you not! She is engaged to Bria. I'm just as stunned as you are," Millie said in all honesty. "You might have turned her out with that tongue of yours; to the point where she don't consider dick as something she'll ever need again in her life. I mean you did put her in the hospital." Omar sat back down in his chair.

"You know this shit is all your fault," he said feeling defeated.

"And that's why I'm going to fix it," Millie said.

"How Millie? How are you going to fix it?" Omar asked unconvinced.

"Because Bria ass ain't no saint! A friend of mine named Skittles strips at Club Assville and she told me that Bria was messing with another stripper that works there by the name of Sugar. Which I'm sure that Tia do not know about, yet!" Omar shook his head, still a little punch drunk from the idea of Tia being a lesbian.

"This is too much. I'm speechless. What the hell can Bria do for her that I can't do ten times better?"

"I'm not sure, but you know a woman knows a woman's body better than a man can ever know it. Maybe her oral skills are out of this world," Millie antagonized.

"I don't give a damn how good her tongue is. She don't have shit on me. I'LL EAT A PUSSY INTO A COMA," Omar screamed causing Millie to feel damp between her legs.

"Well I would love to agree, but I was never fortunate enough to rate your skills. Maybe Tia passed out for some other reason that really had nothing to do with you or her climax. I'm just saying." Omar stood up slowly and then walked around his desk to where Millie sat. He grabbed her under her arm and stood her up. Millie could see the fire in his eyes as he scooped her up off her feet. Millie wrapped her legs around his waist as he walked her back behind his desk. Using his right hand, he swept the contents off his desk onto the floor and gently sat Millie down on it.

"There is no one greater, man or woman," Omar said and then sat down in his chair pulling himself up to his desk and between Millie's legs. "My dick game is vicious and my tongue game is delicious." Omar rolled Millie's skirt up to her waist and then pushed her back flat on his desk. Then he reached down and took off Millie's high heels and pushed her legs up on the desk. Millie's feet sat flat on the desk while her toes wrapped around the edge of the desk. Millie had on a pair of Omar's bubble gum scented panties with the word Goodies etched around the waistband. Omar ran his nose down the crack of her pussy lips and then back up.

"Ummm," Millie moaned as Omar dug his fingers in grabbing the fabric of the panties and began ripping them slowly. He only wanted to rip the crotch area just enough to expose Millie's pussy so he could still smell the bubble gum scent as he dined on her. Millie could not see, nor care less what Omar was doing between her legs. She was just waiting on the first lick to heaven which was not a long wait at all. As soon as he had ripped enough of her panties and he could see her pussy lips, Omar pushed her legs apart as wide as they would go and then let his tongue do the talking. Millie was on her third orgasm in less than ten minutes and she was having trouble completing a sentence. "O-O-O-O-Omar... I-I-I-I-I'm bout, bout, bout, bout to..." The only thing that was on Omar's mind was *"there's no fucking way Bria can eat pussy this good! Can Bria do this, or this? What about this?"*

"I'M CUMMING AGAIN," Millie screamed so loud that Omar's secretary had to hear her, but Omar was not letting up. He dug in deeper with his tongue as Millie's body shook and shivered all across his dripping wet face and chin. Millie was building back up quickly and she felt it before it even came. The one was the one. This was the big O. It started at her toenails and it was now ripping through her knees.

"OOOOOOHHHHHHH!" Millie screamed which was Omar's cue. He let go of her clit from between his lips and then he began rubbing it as fast as he could with two fingers and to make matters even more mind blowing, Omar Goodness darted his tongue from Millie's burning hot pussy to her pussy juiced asshole nonstop. He went back and forth, back and forth until there was nothing, but silence coming from Millie. Her moans and screams were caught somewhere in the back of her throat as she exploded her juices everywhere. Omar felt like he had just gotten hit in the face with a water balloon filled with warm water. Then Millie screamed out again and cried at the same time. She was too weak to move away from Omar's tongue that was flapping like it had a mind of its own.

Using all of the inner strength she had in her body, Millie thrust backwards away from Omar's tongue and fell off of his desk hitting her head on the paperweight that he had pushed off of his desk earlier. Omar jumped up and ran around his desk to find an unconscious Millie laying there with blood coming from the side of her head. Omar ran to his door, yanked it open, and screamed to his secretary, "CALL 911! CALL 911!" He had done it again, OMG!

Millie was given four stitches on the side of her head and then sent home that same night. The words, *mind blowing* was an understatement when she thought about her earlier experience with Omar. Now she was confused. She couldn't decide if she should help Omar get Tia back or if she should make sure that they never got back together.

Assville

M illie sat at the bar taking shots of Patron as she waited for Skittles to come out of the dressing room. She watched the beautiful strippers make the most unattractive men in the club feel like they were gorgeous models and then turn around and get paid for it. Moments later, Skittles walked over wearing a rainbow colored two piece.

"Hey Millie," Skittles said eyeing the crowd for her regulars.

"Hey you! You are looking all fit and in shape." Skittles did a 360 spin showing off her perfectly toned body.

"What are you doing looking for Sugar? Let me find out that she turned you out too," Skittles joked.

"Nah, it's nothing like that. You know my best friend Tia is about to get married to Bria, so I wanted to make sure that she's not playing my girl for no fool. You feel what I'm saying?"

"Well Sugar ass in in love with her some Bria. When Bria come in here, Sugar warned all of us to stay the fuck away from her, but when Bria not around, Sugar be in here acting like a straight whore." Millie took another shot and absorbed all of the information that she needed on Sugar in her head. "There go Sugar right there coming out of the dressing room," Skittles said nodding with her head over towards the dressing room. Then she got up and told Millie that she would be right back.

Millie got up and walked over to where Sugar stood talking to another stripper that resembled Toni Braxton. "Excuse me, I'm kind of new to this environment and I was wondering if you could dance for me, but like in private? I'm kind of shy," Millie said to Sugar in a very innocent and convincing manner.

"Okay honey, come with me. My name is Sugar."

"Hello Sugar. My name is Malika," Millie said. Sugar grabbed a hold of Millie's hand and lead her to one of the club's private booths.

Never Letting Up

Tia was at the gym early Saturday morning doing her regular workout routine with her earplugs pumping out an up-tempo song by Beyonce. She had already broken out into a good sweat. Running on the treadmill kept her body nice and firm and she never went a week without going at it for a few hours. Tia felt someone tap her on the shoulder and without breaking her stride; she turned her head back to find a smiling Omar Goodness. She knew that the tights that she wore did little to stop her ass from bouncing up and down causing her to wonder how long he was behind her; just watching. Tia pressed the stop button and stepped down off the treadmill.

"What the hell are you doing here Omar," she said trying to sound pissed, but she was actually glad to see him. Even though her and Bria had made up, she was still on the fence with that phone call.

"I came to work out," Omar said and then looked down from his feet all the way up to his chest showing Tia that he was dressed for a good sweat.

"So why do I feel like I'm being stalked?"

"Please don't bring up the word stalker," Omar said causing Tia to laugh.

"Oh yeah, we don't need Joy coming from behind the vending machine acting like she came to work out too." Omar shook his head at the thought of Tia's words.

"Tia," Omar said.

"Yes Omar?"

"Please?"

"Please what?" Tia asked confused.

"Please take me back?" Right then and there Omar saw hesitation like she was actually considering it.

"Omar, I've told you over and over again that---..." Omar stopped her in midsentence. He rushed into her so fast that she didn't have time to think. He kissed her with enough passion to make a cold heart turn warm and she kissed him back. The strength of a man was something that Bria could never provide. Then she felt him poking her through his sweats and she almost reached down to caress his dick, but Omar pulled away in the nick of time. "I'm sorry Ms. Fields, but whoever it is that you're about to marry only got you by default and I will never stop until I make you my wife!" Tia looked down at Omar's bulge and then quickly turned her head away. Omar began to back his way to the entrance with both of his hands covering his heart. "I love you Tia," he said and then he was gone. That's when the tears began to cascade down Tia's face because she loved him too.

Up To No Good

It had been almost three weeks and still there was no sign of Sugar. Bria had texted her here and there, but she never got a response so she decided to call her.

"Hello," Sugar answered on the third ring without the excitement in the voice that Bria was used to hearing.

"That's all I get is a hello and I haven't heard from you in almost a month?"

"I can't really talk right now."

"Why? Who the hell are you with that you can't talk to me, Sugar?" Bria asked sounding frustrated.

"I'll call you back. Just give me a few."

"No, I..." (CLICK) Sugar ended the call leaving Bria's heart crushed and confused.

Sugar rolled over and wrapped her arms around her new lover. "Who was that?" Millie asked feeling the comfort of Sugar's body wrapped around hers.

"Remember my ex Bria, the one that's about to get married?"

"Yeah, what did she want?" Millie asked.

"Who the hell knows! That girl is so confused Malika."

"That reminds me, you never showed me the pictures of her."

"You sure you can handle it? They are very explicit," Sugar warned.

"I think so baby. They might even turn me on," Millie said grinding her ass into Sugar.

"Listen at you, my little shy Malika is turning into a little freak and I love it," Sugar said smiling.

"You did it to me," Millie whispered.

Sugar grabbed her phone and went into her pictures. Then she passed Millie her phone. Millie scrolled through photo after photo of Bria and Sugar engaging in a whole lot of pussy licking and nipple pinching sex.

"Ohhhh baby, this is turning me on," Millie said turning flat on her back and grabbing Sugar's head and pushing it down between her legs. Sugar began to slowly lick on Millie's clit as Millie continued to look at the photos; well at least that's what Sugar thought Millie was doing. Millie was actually e-mailing the photos to her own yahoo account. "Ummmm," Millie moaned.

Game Recognize Game

Bria and Apple walked through the mall window shopping. Well, that's what they appeared to be doing, but in all actuality Bria had a lot on her mind and who was better to vent to than Apple's ratchet ass.

"I'm telling you, something is not right with Tia. She's been acting so distant lately and I'm starting to second guess this whole marriage thing," Bria said.

"Maybe she's getting tired of your bullshit Bria," Apple suggested.

"I don't know. I think she's seeing someone else."

"Guilty conscience, huh? That's what karma does to a bitch! Ohhh look at those shoes girl! Let's go in here so I can price them," Apple said. The two ladies walked into the shoe store only to find Sugar and another stripper by the name of Flexy in there buying shoes.

"Wow! What a pleasant surprise," Bria exclaimed.

"That it is. How are you doing sexy," Sugar replied.

"I would be doing just fine if I only knew why you were avoiding me."

"Don't I know you?" Apple asked Flexy.

Maybe. You ever been to club Assville?"

"Oh shit! Flexy right?" Apple said all hyped up like she was meeting a celebrity.

"That's meeee," Flexy said.

Bria pulled Sugar to the side to see what was really going on. "So what' up Sugar? Is there something you want to tell me?"

"Uhhh, no!"

"Is that who's been getting my time?" Bria asked gesturing towards Flexy.

"No, but if it was, I don't feel like I owe you an explanation. In fact, holla at me when you're done playing house! Flexy, come on. We out!" Sugar stormed out of the store and didn't bother to even look back once.

After Sugar and Flexy left the shoe store, Apple smiled and decided to joke Bria. "I could hook you up with Kilo's friend Bo-Netta."

"Ugh, I rather you don't, but now you see what I'm saying, right. I think my shit falling off."

"Bitch, please! Let's get some new shoes and then hit the club tonight. I bet you that bitches will be all over you as usual," Apple said a little too loud for Bria's taste.

"Hell no! I'm taking my ass home to Tia! I can't lose her Apple. That's my heart, right there."

What's On Your Mind

"*Oh yes Omar.... Fuck this pussy! Give me that dick*," Tia thought to herself as she played with herself under the comforter. "Mmmmm... mmmm... Oh yessss," she said out loud as she felt herself about to release a powerful orgasm. She rubber her clit faster as her toes began to curl up and her ass started to raise up off the bed until she was interrupted.

"Ti-Ti, are you hungry baby? I got you some food," Bria screamed.

"*DAMN!*" Tia screamed to herself. Bria was home and she just totally fucked up Tia's nut and she was beyond pissed.   Seconds later Bria entered the bedroom.

"Did you hear me baby? I brought you some food."

"Oh no, I didn't hear you," Tia lied without taking her eyes off of the flat screen.   Bria felt the cold shoulder.

"Well?" Bria asked.

"Well what?"

"Are you hungry or not?"

"No, not really. Just put it in the microwave. I'll heat it up later," Tia said still not taking her eyes off of the T.V. Bria stood there and stared at her for a whole two minutes, but Tia refused to look in her direction.

"Hey, what's on your mind?" Bria asked.

"A lot," Tia said still not looking at Bria.

Bria walked over to the T.V. and turned it off. Then she climbed upon the bed directly in front of Tia and said, "I'm listening."

Tia let out a loud sigh. "I'm dealing with a lot of trust issues due to my past relationships and ever since I answered your phone, I don't trust you either!" Tia grabbed her box of tissues from beside the bed and dabbed the corner of her eyes with one.

"What is love without trust, Ti-Ti?"

"Misery," Tia replied wiping tears from her eyes.

"Wowww! That's a nasty word. So are you miserable being in this relationship with me," Bria asked grabbing a tissue for herself because her eyes had started to well up.

"No, I love you. It's just that I thought dealing with a woman would eliminate all of my issues and other desires."

"Other desires?" Bria asked quickly. "What other desires do you have because whatever they are, I'll be more than happy to make sure they are met regardless of what they are."

Tia burst into tears. "You don't understand Bria. You just don't understand." Bria wrapped her arms around Tia who was now sobbing uncontrollably.

"Whatever it is, we will get through it baby," Bria said.

Love vs. Love

Once again Omar watched Joy leave from work and then waited for Millie to exit the building. Just as usual, about ten minutes after Joy left, Millie came out of the building. This time Omar was riding in his black Masarti wearing an Armani suit. Millie began to get wet on sight. She walked right up to Omar's car and got inside. Whatever type of cologne he was wearing, the scent was so intoxicating that she closed her eyes and laid her head back on the seat and just inhaled.

"How's your head feeling?" Omar asked pushing Millie's hair to the side to see the scar on her head.

"It's healing. They took the stitches out two days ago."

"I'm sorry about that. I didn't..."

Millie cut him off. "Don't you dare apologize for that wonderful experience. That's what I get for underestimating your skills." Omar was flattered, but that's not what he was here for.

"So you said that you got something I might want to see."

"Show me yours and I'll show you mine," Millie joked, but Omar didn't laugh.

He was ready to get down to business. He was serious about trying to win Tia back so he didn't have time for Millie's games. "What do you have for me Millie?"

Millie rolled her eyes and then dug her phone out of her purse. After pressing a few things on her touch screen, she passed Omer her phone showing him the photos of Bria and Sugar going at it. One photo showed Bria with her chin dripping wet. The look on her face said it all. Not only did she bring Sugar to a squirting orgasm, but the look on her face said she loved the taste just as much as Sugar loved the feeling.

"May I?" Omar asked pointing to Millie's phone. "Sure be my guest," Millie said. Omar e-mailed the pictures to his own e-mail account and then erased them out of Millie's phone. "You did good Millie. Thank you!"

"Thank you? That's all I get?"

Omar unzipped his zipper and pulled his dick out. He grabbed Millie by the back of her head trying to degrade her, but instead of Millie feeling degraded, she was turned on. "You got ten minutes. I got shit to do," Omar said sounding a little frustrated.

"I only need five," Millie said and then licked her lips. Omar shoved her head down in his lap and then turned the music up. It turned out that Millie only needed three minutes and eight seconds. Omar gripped his wood grain steering wheel with every piece of strength he had as he unloaded almost a half of pint of cum down Millie's throat. How she got the pictures never even crossed his mind. The only thing on his mind at that moment was how good Millie had sucked him off.

Game Time

Omar Goodness sat at the bar in the upscale 40/40 club watching the Monday night football game. The football game was actually watching him because his mind was elsewhere. Omar didn't want to hurt Tia just to get her back. He wanted her to want him. He didn't want to be the rebound guy, but the little devil that sat on his shoulder whispering in his ear was saying, *"Fuck that! All is fare in love and war!"* While the little angle on his other

PANTY RIPPER

shoulder was saying, "*Build the foundation of the relationship with love and admiration, not with pain and heartache!*"

"Excuse me," Omar's thoughts were interrupted by two lovely looking redbone twins.

"Yes ladies, how may I help you?" Omar asked politely.

"My name is Vicky and this is my sister Veronica. We were just wondering if you were Omar Goodness?"

"Yes ladies, that would be me."

"I TOLD YOU!" Vicky screamed at her sister and then said, "All we wear is Goodies. Your panties are so comfortable."

"And sexy," Veronica added with a smile. "Can we take a picture with you, please?"

"Yeah sure. Why not? Let's do it," Omar said. The twins took position on Omar's left and right side and stopped a waitress as she was walking by and asked her to take a picture of them.

"At the count of three, everybody say Goodies," Vicky said sounding very excited. After the waitress took the picture Veronica said, "If you ever need a set of hot twins to model your panties just give us a call. You should see us in a thong." Then she winked at Omar and slid him her number. The twins walked away and Omar watched as their round asses switched with every step they took. Vicky turned around to see if

150

Omar was watching and she made the phone sign with her thumb and pinky and then mouthed the words, "*Call me.*"

Even though the twins were a beautiful distraction, Omar's thoughts went right back to Tia and how he wanted to play this situation out. After a few more drinks, Omar thought of something that just might work and if it didn't, then he would have to move on to drastic measures.

Forcing Hands

Getting Bria's cell phone number was a piece of cake for Omar. Millie was the one who had to put in the work by letting Sugar ride her face until she squirted cum all over her face making it a milky mess. After that mind blowing session, Sugar went straight to sleep. Sugar was actually snoring when Millie slid out of the bed and snuck Bria's number out of her phone.

Two days later Omar was sitting at his desk feeling good about what he had just did. Now all he had to do was sit back and wait before he made his next move. This was becoming one big game of Chess and he was moving in for the checkmate.

Sacrifice Your Queen

Bria's hands began to shake as she stared at the pictures of her an Sugar that was sent to her phone moments ago with the following text message attached to them...

You have 24 hours to end your relationship with Tia. If not these pics will be forwarded to her.

Bria tried her best to think of something that could refute the photos, but how could she? There was no way of claiming that the photos were taken a while back due to the fact of the engagement ring that glitter on her hand in each photo. Tia was at work and she was due to be home in a few hours so with her eyes full of tears, Bria began to pack her personal belongings in two large suitcases. After she finished, she sat down and wrote Tia a *Dear Jane letter*.

To the love of my life,

Tia first let me start this heart wrenching letter off by saying I do not deserve to have someone as good as you in my life. I have took your trust and love for granted and I'm ashamed to the point that I'd rather write you this letter than to look you in your eyes and cause you anymore pain. The trust issues that you were battling with ware your intuition letting you know that things were not right which is totally my fault. There's so much I want to say, but I'm really having a hard time breathing as I write this letter. Just know that in a perfect world, you would make any man or woman the perfect wife. If you could ever find it in your beautiful heart to forgive me, which I can honestly say I do not deserve. I t will be a blessing that I will cherish for the rest of my life.

I love you beautiful,

Brianna Jones

Bria left the engagement ring and a photo of her and Tia that they took on vacation on the top of the letter. Then she left Tia's apartment in tears with two Louis Vuitton suitcases.

PANTY RIPPER

Backfire

One Week Later

This was the third day in a row that Omar sat posted outside of Tia's job. It was already twenty minutes past her lunch break hour and she still had not exited the building. Omar could not understand it so he walked inside of the small law office. He marched right up to the pretty white secretary and spoke.

"Excuse me; is Ms. Tia Fields in today?"

"I'm sorry sir, but Ms. Fields quit last week." Omar was floored. He thanked the secretary and then turned to leave. "Excuse me, sir?"

"Yes?"

"Did anyone ever tell you that you look like Omar Goodness?" she asked with a smile.

"Unfortunately yes. I heard he was a real jerk though," Omar stated sourly and then left out of the building.

For the rest of the day Omar was losing his mind trying to find Tia's whereabouts. He even tried her phone number and that too was temporarily disconnected. He sat alone in his beautiful home wondering if he was the cause of Tia's disappearance and her phone being cut off.

Bria the Cheater

Omar Goodness was not the only one feeling the effects of Tia's absence. Bria sat in Olive Garden with Apple nursing a glass of wine as her food sat there on the table untouched and getting cold. Apple devoured her food and kept looking at Bria's as they talked.

"So what did Sugar say about the picture?" Apple asked.

"She denied it. So I asked her who else had access to her phone and of course she flipped out saying that I must think that she is desperate for me to accuse her of some shit like that.

"I don't know Bria. The whole thing sounds a little shady to me and you know I'm the queen of shady. I know one thing, all this drama got me hungry as hell. Are you gonna eat those shrimp?" Bria passed Apple the platter of fried jumbo shrimp.

"I haven't heard..."

"Not to cut you off, but please pass me that red sauce too," Apple said cutting Bria off.

Bria passed Apple the cocktail sauce and said, "Like I was saying, I haven't heard anything from Tia since the day I left."

"Girl, let me try that white sauce," Apple said with a mouthful of shrimp.

"It's called tartar sauce Apple. Are you even listening to me?" Bria snapped.

"Umm, hmm," Apple said.

"Did I tell you that she quit her job?"

"No you didn't, but look you can't beat yourself up about it because you knew you wasn't ready to be tied down anyway. She was the one forcing the whole marriage thing. I'm an advocate for lesbian relationships, but all that marriage nonsense is not what I believe in," Apple explained as she ate.

"Well, I don't agree. Marriage doesn't have a gender restriction. It's all about love," Bria said.

"Well love should have brought your ass home all them nights you spent with Sugar! Pass me one of them breadsticks," Apple said trying to pick food out of her teeth with a fork.

"I still think Sugar is behind all of this. Like whoelse would want to see me and Tia separated. I know one thing for sure, when I do find out who did this, it's going to be hell to pay!"

"PAY! PAY WHAT! I THOUGT YOU WAS TREATING," Apple yelled looking like she was ready to run out of Olive Garden.

Millie was back at Ms. Lee's nail salon trying to find out anything that she could about Tia's disappearance. Omar was promising her the best panty ripping, ass smacking, hair pulling, pussy sucking, fuck fest of her life if she could locate Tia. That was all the motivation that Millie needed to go on a hunt.

"You know they saying that my friend do not lay down with women anymore, right Ms. Lee," Millie stated.

"You late news," Ms. Lee said as she filed Millie's nails. "Friend come here, no wedding ring on." Millie played it off like she was shocked.

"Wowww! I can't believe it! Who did she come with to get her nails done?"

"Friend come with mother. Very nice lady."

Of course Millie thought, "Yes Ms. Fields is a very nice lady. She's like a second mother to me." That's when Millie remembered that Tia would always spend time with her mother whenever she had personal problems. Millie had to drag her back home a few times throughout the years. Millie was excited to know that Omar was going to ravish her pussy once more when she told him where Tia was staying.

Mrs. Independent

Tia Fields walked around the exotic toy store in search of a body spasming device that would keep her mind off of missing Bria's tongue. That's how she ended up in the toy store. Tia was so damn horny sitting around her mother's house that she had to get out and find something to do. She had been molesting the showerhead twice daily and even that was starting to lose its magic.

"Hello Miss, is there anything in particular that you are looking for," a tall gentleman that obviously worked there asked. Tia was a little embarrassed. Her freaky side was always locked behind closed doors so being all out in the open with it caught her off guard.

"Uhh, I-I-I was looking for something," Tia stuttered. *(Her mind was saying, just spit it out.)* "Something powerful," she blurted out.

"Okay, well do you prefer deep penetration or clitoral stimulation?" the salesman asked causing Tia to blush.

"Clitoral stimulation," Tia said.

"I think I have the perfect stimulator for you. These guys are new, but so far the feedback has been awesome," the salesman said. Tia walked with the salesman to the back of the store where she passed enough sex toys to make her pussy throb. The way she was feeling right now, she could turn them all on at once and put them all over her body.

"This is it right here. It's called The Plumber," the salesman said.

"And why do they call it that?" Tia asked.

"They call it the plumber because it will cause a flood! If you know what I mean?" the salesman said with a smile.

"I'll take it," Tia said and just like that she made her purchase and headed back to her mother's house. She damn near ran up the stairs to her old bedroom and locked the door behind her. Tia ripped the box off of The Plumber the way kids tear wrapping paper off of a Christmas present. After peeling out of her clothes and jumping into her bed, Tia turned The Plumber on and placed it on her clit.

"Ohhh shit! What the hell? OHHHH," she screamed as a surge rippled through her body. For the next two hours, Tia cursed and came so many times that she lost count. She was so drained that she forgot to turn The Plumber off before she fell asleep. As she slept peacefully, The Plumber buzzed on the bed beside her.

The Next Day

Tia woke up the aroma of her mother's cooking. She smelled banana nut pancakes and bacon that that was her favorite. She couldn't wait to get downstairs to sink her teeth in one of those pancakes. As she sat up in the bed, she heard voices. One of the voices was her mother and the other voice was the voice of a man.

"*Who the hell is mama cooking breakfast for?*" she said to herself. "Let me find out that Stella got her groove back," Tia mumbled as Tia crawled her weak legs out of bed. After washing up and brushing her teeth, she headed down the stairs. Tia turned the corner and walked into the kitchen and she almost cursed in front of her God fearing mother.

"What the f---," she screamed. Tia could not believe her eyes. Omar Goodness was standing over her mother's stove frying bacon and her mom was smiling from ear to ear.

"Tia why didn't you tell me that you were friends with Omar Goodness?" her mother asked with her voice full of excitement. Tia screwed her face up. She didn't like the way her mother said the word *Goodness*.

"Good morning Tia we made you your favorite breakfast," Omar smiled holding a spatula in his hand. Tia was fuming mad.

"Good morning ma," she said sounding real stink. "Omar, can I have a word with you?" Omar thought he saw steam coming from her ears and nose.

"You sure you don't want to eat first?" he asked.

"NOW!" Tia screamed and then stormed out of the kitchen.

"Call me if you need me," Tia's mother whispered.

Omar walked into the living room looking a little nervous and turned on at the sight of Tia's sexy mean look with her nostrils flared up.

"Are you crazy or what?" Tia snapped. She was so mad that she could literally kill Omar right now.

"Crazy about you," Omar replied in a smooth tone.

"Omar this is borderline stalker insanity! You can't show up at someone's mother's house and cook breakfast and converse like you've known them your whole life."

"Tia I love you," Omar admitted. Tia's mouth fell open in shock. This was the second time she heard these words come out of Omar's mouth.

"What are you talking about?" Tia mumbled.

Omar shook his head. "You make me do crazy shit like this. I don't know what else to do to prove to you that if you give me a chance I will make you the happiest woman in America. Millie tricked me. If not we probably would be on our honeymoon somewhere and you'd probably be fat and pregnant, but still beautiful, and I'd be so happy that everybody would literally want to slap the smile off of my face." Tia giggled at Omar's last statement, but she still was not ready to let him off the hook.

"How the hell did you find out where my mother lived anyway?"

"I just followed my heart."

Tia was not in a joking mood. She was just about to let Omar have it when their conversation was interrupted by a knock on the front door. Just when Tia thought her morning couldn't get any crazier she snatched the door open and there stood Bria wearing the saddest puppy face that Tia had ever seen. Tia was at a loss for words. She tried to say something but nothing was coming out.

"I miss you beautiful," Bria said and then dropped her head.

"*Think, think, think Tia,*" Tia told herself. She could not let Omar find out that she was engaged to Bria and not a man. Not that she was ashamed, Tia just did not want him in her personal business.

"Tia... Tia, who was that at the door?" Tia's mother yelled as she walked into the living room heading straight to the open door. "Heeeey baby get in here and give me a hug," she yelled. Bria entered the house and had to do a double take when she saw Omar Goodness standing there.

"Hello Mrs. Fields I didn't know y'all had company. I should have called first," Bria said with her voice cracking a little. Tia was stuck on stupid. She knew that Bria knew about Omar and the whole panty ripping fainting situation. What she didn't know was that Omar already knew about their relationship and engagement and it was quite obvious that Tia's mother didn't know anything about this whole ordeal.

"Hush now Bria, you know you are family. Do you know Tia's friend Omar Goodness? He's the one that makes the lingerie," Ms. Fields whispered as she hugged Bria tightly.

"Actually I do know him. Hello Omar. What a surprise to find you here," Bria said never taking her eyes off of Tia.

"Hey Bria, it's been a long time. You know my boy Askari always ask about you."

"Well let's eat breakfast before the food gets cold. Omar here made Tia her favorite breakfast. Wasn't that sweet of him Bria?"

"Very," Bria replied clearly fuming over her own incorrect assumptions. Bria's first thought was to decline Ms. Fields offer, but then she decided against it when Omar grabbed Ms. Fields and said. "Yes let's eat,"

"Okay why not," Bria said in a condescending tone.

"It's not what you think," Tia mumbled to Bria as they walked into the kitchen. After everyone was seated Ms. Fields took control. "Okay everyone grab a hand so I can bless the food. It just so happens that seating at the table allowed both Bria and Omar to hold one of Tia's hands and one of the mother's.

Ms. Field's cleared her throat and then took them to church. "Thank you Lord for this blessing you bestowed upon us this morning Lord. Without you

Lord this beautiful day would not be possible and I know my Lord, so I see that you are putting the pieces together as we sit here for my baby to walk down that...."

"Ma!" Tia screamed cutting her mother off. "Amen, amen now let's eat." Tia shook her head in embarrassment.

Ms. Fields and Omar seemed to be the only two with appetites. Bria had an appetite for destruction. "Tia why aren't you eating? Your man went through all this hard work for you and you are just going to sit there and not eat?" Bria asked casually.

"So Bria how many pairs of Goodies do you own?" Ms. Fields asked catching everyone off guard including Omar.

"Ma is that a question you should be asking after you just blessed the food?"

"Hush Tia, I'm just trying to get your friend the hook up."

Omar laughed, but Bria and Tia did not. "Baby can you pass me the syrup?" Omar asked Tia. He made sure he put extra emphasis the word baby. Tia looked up at him with a grimace and then picked up her fork and picked at her food.

"Tia, did you hear Omar ask for the syrup?" Ms. Fields asked. Tia's reaction shocked everyone at the table when she burst into tears and then screamed. "I'm nobody's baby!" She threw her fork on top of her plate and ran upstairs to her room.

"Jesus please help my child," Ms. Fields mumbled as Omar and Bria both got up from the table in pursuit of the woman that they both loved. Tia lay on her stomach with her face buried in her pillow crying her eyes out. Bria and Omar entered the room and they both were heartbroken at the sight. Bria sat on the bed and rubbed Tia's back.

"Ti-Ti, don't cry beautiful. We are going to get through this all of this," Bria pleaded.

"I'm here for you baby just let me take care of you and I promise you there will only be happy tears from now on," Omar offered.

"Why are y'all here? Just leave me the fuck alone! Get out!" Tia screamed in between sobs.

"Baby I'm just..."

"Get out both of y'all!" Tia barked.

Omar and Bria had no other choice but to leave Tia to herself. Once outside of Tia's mother's house they engaged in a small dispute that would be the first of the tug of war for Tia Fields' affection.

"How dare you try to get back with her after you fucked her best friend? The same best friend that got your name tattooed on her ass," Bria spat

"Don't stand here talking to me like your shit is squeaky clean Mrs. Bria the diva because it's not. See the difference between me and you is this, Millie convinced me that Tia was back with her ex so I slipped up and played myself, but youuu..." he pointed his finger at her.

"But me what?"

"You out here sleeping with nasty ass strippers then going right back home to lay up with Tia. So which one is worst?" Omar asked catching Bria off guard.

"Omar please! No matter what you say or do she'll never choose you over me and that's a fact." Bria said confidently.

"Oh really?" Omar asked with a smirk on his face. Omar always loved a challenge.

"Yes really."

"Interesting..."

"Very..."

"Well I guess we'll have to see about that," Omar stated.

"You cannot compare your one night with her to our one year relationship so don't hold your breath playa. That's my pussy!"

"Well let me take it off your hands, since you've already got one," Omar said hitting below the belt.

"Yes I do have one and guess what? Tia loves it and she is actually addicted to the taste and scent of it," Bria said with a smirk.

"She might be, but she'll never forget about Omar Goodness! Remember who sent that pussy to the E.R; me, not you!"

Scheming

"**S**o how are things with you and Omar?" Bria asked knowing she would get some sort of delusional answer and she did.

"Oh things are very well. We have our moments, but what relationships don't? I wouldn't be surprised if marriage was somewhere in our future," Joy said beaming with pride.

"Congratulations girl! You deserve it. You better send me an invite," Bria played right along with Joy's nonsense. "Joy do you mind if I ask you a personal question?"

"Not at all what's up?"

"Is it true what they say about Omar Goodness? Is he like really a panty ripping beast or is that too personal? Joy looked around like she was about to reveal a top secret government mission and then whispered.

"It's true and let me tell you this; it's an experience that cannot be compared to anything else in this world. It's something about hearing your panties getting ripped off that turns you into a voluntary sex slave," Joy confessed. Bria covered her mouth playing the role of being shocked.

"Girl you need to get that shit on film so when he's not around you can watch it."

"I wish, but Omar would never go for that."

"He doesn't even have to know girl. Set you up one of those nanny cams. Joy do you think it would have the same effect if it was a woman that ripped another woman's panties off?"

"Why you thinking about trying it on Tia?" Joy asked with a sneaky smile on her face.

"Look at you all freaky on the down low. Omar Goodness done turned your ass out and if you must know, yes I am thinking about trying it on Tia." Joy seemed more excited about it than Bria.

"Well you got to do it right. It's all about execution and timing okay?"

"See that's why I need to get it on camera, so I can see exactly how to do it." Joy looked around the Starbucks to make sure the FEDS or the CIA wasn't listening to their conversation.

"Okay I'll do it!"

Plotting

While Bria sat around scheming on assassinating Omar's character, Omar had his feet kicked up on his desk plotting on different ways to win Tia over. He wasn't worried about Bria. The photo he had of her and Sugar was all evidence he would need if he had to resort to a plan B. Omar figured the best way to get to Tia's heart was using her own emotions against her and he knew the perfect way to do it. He had to provide a stress reliever in her life. Omar picked up his phone and dialed Tia's mother's number.

"Hello Ms. Fields, this is Omar how are you doing?"

"Heyyy Omar," Ms. Fields screamed. "I'm doing just fine. I'm telling you my God is good."

"Yes he is, but listen," Omar said quickly changing the subject. "I want to send you and Tia on a trip to Jamaica, just a little early vacation."

"Oh my God are you serious Omar?" she screamed causing Omar to remove the phone from his ear.

"Yes I'm dead serious. Tia's been going through a lot lately and I just want her to go somewhere nice and peaceful to get some relaxation, but there's one thing I need you to do for me Ms. Fields."

"Anything baby, you just name it and the Lord be my witness it'll get done."

"Okay Tia's kind of mad with me right now so I don't want her to know that I'm sending y'all on the trip. I want you to tell her that you're paying for everything okay?"

"Okay Omar no problem at all."

2 weeks later

Tia was back at her apartment feeling lonely. It was her twenty-fifth birthday and since it fell on a Tuesday, going out to enjoy it at a club was not going to happen. Tia heard a knock at her door. She was in no mood for any company so she dragged her feet to answer it. Tia looked through the peep hole and her heart skipped a beat. She opened the door slowly.

"Happy birthday my moon," Omar Goodness said as he stood there holding a dozen long stem roses.

"Happy birthday beautiful," Bria said standing next to Omar holding a big white fluffy teddy bear. Tia let them in her apartment, thanked them both for their gifts, and then she was pretty much at a loss for words.

"We decided to put our differences to the side for your birthday. It's obvious that we both love you so I guess we are going to have to share you," Omar said with his signature smile.

Sh-share me what do you mean?"

"This is what we mean," Bria said and then walked over to Tia and kissed her passionately. Tia's mind went blank and she got lost in the lusciousness of Bria's lips. Tia totally forgot that Omar was in the room until she felt his body press into her back. Omar reached his hands around her and rubbed her breast through her shirt. She felt his dick poking her on her ass and she felt herself getting wet in between her thighs.

"Ummm... What is y'all doing?"

"Don't talk beautiful. Just enjoy... mmm... happy birthday," Bria whispered in Tia's ear and then stuck her tongue in it. Tia's knee's buckled. Omar caught her by the waist before she slid to the floor. He picked her up and threw her over his shoulder like a sack of potatoes.

"Bring her sexy ass upstairs," Bria demanded. After climbing the steps they entered the bedroom. Omar laid Tia on the bed. She was wearing a wife beater with no bra underneath so her nipples were reaching for the stars. Tia had a pair of ass hugging jeggings on. Omar climbed on one side of the bed and Bria crawled on the other side. They both grabbed at Tia's wife beater and began to rip it off. Next, they each took a nipple in each of their mouth and Tia spilled inside of her panties. After ten minutes of sucking all over Tia's titties they yanked her jeggings off one leg at a time.

"Wait... Wait... I can't handle both of y'all... Tooooo... Much... This is too much!" Tia panted, but they did not stop. The sight of Tia wearing a thong by Goodies blew Omar's mind.

"You ready?" he asked Bria. Who responded with a wink of her eye. They went at Tia's panties with all teeth, tugging and ripping at the same damn time until she laid there in the nude.

"Have you ever had your whole pussy ate at one time beautiful?" Bria asked. Tia was confused with the question so she just shook her head no for the hell of it. Bria laid flat on the bed next to Tia then said, "Get on top." Tia crawled on top of Bria in the 69 position and without hesitation the pussy slurping and sucking began.

"Ummm... Hmm.... Hmmm... Umm...," Bria moaned inside of Tia's pussy. Omar came up from behind. Tia was in the perfect doggy style position with Bria underneath her sucking on her clit. Omar did not waste any time. He dived his face into Tia's hot creamy pussy and tried to suck her insides out. Tia screamed in ecstasy.

Haaaah... Oooooh, oh, oh yes!" Tia was making noises that could not be explained in the English language until she began to cry for help. "H-H-H-Help me! Somebody help me... Ummm..." Less than a minute later there was a combustion of juices running down Omar's face and landing on Bria's face. Tia's body spasmed every tenth of a second. If she was even able to think at that point she wouldn't believe that she was engaging in a threesome with Omar Goodness and Brianna Jones. Tia's mind was so gone that Omar slipped the head of his throbbing dick in her over flooded hot box while Bria still had her clit clamped between her lips.

"Oh shit! Oh shit! O-O-O-Omar!" she screamed as he started a slow, long, powerful stroke inside of her tightness. Tia's pussy literally wrapped itself around the dick and squeezed it.

"Who's pussy is this!?" Omar asked as he forcefully smacked Tia's ass.

"Yours!" she cried out. "Omar it's yours!"

"Who's is it!?" Bria asked and then quickly gave Tia's clit a nice loud slurp.

"Brianna's... Oh God it's Brianna's!" Tia shouted.

"Who's?" Omar screamed as he dug deeper.

"Omar's!"

"Who's!?"

"Brianna's! Ohhhh shit, I'm about to cum... Y'all about to make me pass out!" Tia screamed as she began to feel light headed. "I-I-I-I-I'm coming!" Immediately everything went dark. Tia could not see anything. She felt this feeling when Omar made her faint. She tried to shake it off, but she couldn't and then it happened. Tia's body began to fall to the side and as soon as she hit the bed she woke up out of her dream. Tia's eyes adjusted to the hotel room lighting and then she realized where she was. She was a vacation in Jamaica with her mother who was somewhere laid up on the beach. Tia placed her hands between her legs and she could feel that her juices had soaked through her panties and ran down her thighs

This some bullshit!" she thought as she shook her head, thinking about her dream. Tia laid there thinking too long and her horny little inner person started to scream and curse her hell out. Luckily she brought her Plumber with her. She retrieved it from her suitcase and got back in the bed and climaxed over and over, and over, again thinking about her dream.

"Who's is it!?"

"OMAR'S!"

"WHO'S!?"

"BRIANNA'S!"

TO BE CONTINUED......

The Panty Ripper 3 "Tug of War"
COMING SOON!!

Books by Good2Go Authors on Our Bookshelf

Good2Go Films Presents

To order books, please fill out the order form below:
To order films please go to *www.good2gofilms.com*

Name: _____

Address: _____

City: _____ State: _____ Zip Code: _____

Phone: _____

Email: _____

Method of Payment: ☐ Check ☐ VISA ☐ MASTERCARD

Credit Card#: _____

Name as it appears on card: _____

Signature: _____

Item Name	Price	Qty	Amount
He Loves Me, He Loves You Not - Mychea	$14.99		
He Loves Me, He Loves You Not 2 - Mychea	$14.99		
Married To Da Streets – Silk White	$14.99		
My Boyfriend's Wife - Mychea	$14.99		
Never Be The Same – Silk White	$14.99		
Stranded – Silk White	$14.99		
Slumped – Jason Brent	$14.99		
Tears of a Hustler - Silk White	$14.99		
Tears of a Hustler 2 - Silk White	$14.99		
Tears of a Hustler 3 - Silk White	$14.99		
Tears of a Hustler 4- Silk White	$14.99		
Tears of a Hustler 5 – Silk White	$14.99		
The Teflon Queen – Silk White	$14.99		
The Teflon Queen 2 – Silk White	$14.99		
The Teflon Queen – 3 – Silk White	$14.99		
Young Goonz – Reality Way	$14.99		
Subtotal:			
Tax:			
Shipping (Free) U.S. Media Mail:			
Total:			

Make Checks Payable To:
Good2Go Publishing
7311 W Glass Lane
Laveen, AZ 85339

CPSIA information can be obtained at www.ICGtesting.com
Printed in the USA
LVOW10s1155240615

443675LV00001B/86/P